the knife and the butterfly

ASHLEY HOPE PÉREZ

carolrhoda LAB
MINNEAPOLIS

Text copyright © 2012 by Ashley Hope Pérez

Carolrhoda Lab™ is a trademark of Lerner Publishing Group, Inc.

Carolrhoda Lab™
An imprint of Carolrhoda Books
A division of Lerner Publishing Group, Inc.
241 First Avenue North
Minneapolis, MN 55401 U.S.A.

Website address: www.lernerbooks.com

Main body text set in Janson Text 11/15.
Typeface provided by Linotype AG.

Library of Congress Cataloging-in-Publication Data

Pérez, Ashley Hope.
    The knife and the butterfly / by Ashley Hope Pérez.
        p.   cm.
    Summary: After a brawl with a rival gang, sixteen-year-old Azael, the
son of illegal Salvadoran immigrants and a member of Houston's MS-13
gang, wakes up in an unusual juvenile detention center where he is forced
to observe another inmate through a one-way mirror.
    ISBN: 978–0–7613–6156–5 (trade hard cover : alk. paper)
    [1. Juvenile delinquency—Fiction. 2. Juvenile detention homes—
Fiction. 3. Gangs—Fiction. 4. Salvadoran Americans—Fiction.] I. Title.
PZ7.P4255Kn 2012
[Fic]—dc23   2011021236

Manufactured in the United States of America
1 – SB – 12/31/11

To my boys.
Los quiero mucho.

CHAPTER 1: NOW

I'm standing inches from a wall, staring at a half-finished piece. Even though I'm too close to read what it says, I know it's my work. I run my hands over the black curves outlined in silver. I lean in and sniff. Nothing, not a whiff of fumes. When did I start this? It doesn't matter; I'll finish it now. I start to shake the can in my hand, but all I hear is a hollow rattle. I toss the can down and reach for another, then another. Empty. They're all empty.

I wake up with that all-over shitty feeling you get the day after a rumble. Head splitting, guts twisted. All that's left of my dream is a memory of black and silver. I sit up, thinking about snatching the baggie from under the couch and going to the back lot for a joint before Pelón can bust my balls for smoking his weed.

Except then I realize I'm not at Pelón's. I'm on this narrow cot with my legs all tangled up in a raggedy-ass blanket. It's dark except for a fluorescent flicker from behind me. I get loose of the covers and take four steps one way before I'm up against another concrete wall. Six steps the other way, and I'm bumping into the shitter in the corner. There's a sink right by it. No mirror. Drain bolted into the concrete floor. I can make out words scrawled in Sharpie on the wall to one side of the cot: WELCUM HOME FOOL. I turn around, already half-knowing what I'm going to see.

Bars. Through them, I take in the long row of cells just like this one. I'm in lockup. Shit, juvie again? It's only been four months since I got out of Houston Youth Village. Village, my ass.

I sit back down on the cot and try to push through the fog in my brain from the shit we smoked yesterday. Thing is, I've got no memory of getting brought in here. It's like I want to replay that part, but my brain's a jacked-up DVD player that skips back again and again to the same damn scene, the last thing I can remember right.

We're cruising through the Montrose looking for some fools who'd been messing with Javi's stepsister. We've got this ghetto-ass van that Javi bought off his aunt, and the whole time he's driving he's hitting a bottle of Jack and trashing the punks who called his sister a ho. Pelón's in the front seat, and me, my brother Eddie, plus Mono, Cucaracha, Chuy, Greñas, and three other homeboys are smashed in the back. We're sitting on top of bricks and chains and bats and all the other shit Javi keeps there. All the way, I'm thinking that by the time we get out of the van I'm going to have chains imprinted on my ass from sitting on them so long. There's a knot in my guts. Don't matter how many battles I've been in, I get it every time. But I know as soon as we hit the ground it'll turn into a rush.

"Where the hell are these fools?" I call up to Javi.

"Tranquilo, culero. We'll find them soon," he says, passing the bottle to us in the back.

"Watch for the red and brown," Pelón says, all businesslike.

Greñas lights up a fat joint, sucks on it hard. Everybody's joking and taking hits when Javi sees the beat-up green Caddy his stepsister told him about. He floors it and noses the van right up to the tail of the car. Three dudes in the back throw up their hand sign.

The Caddy flies through stop signs, swerving like a dog with an ass full of wasps.

"Come on, let's ride them bitches!" Mono says.

Javi floors it, and we lurch through a red light.

"Easy, cabrón!" I shout over the horns. "We can't kick their asses if we're dead!"

Javi laughs crazy. "Stop being a pussy, pussy!"

The Caddy pulls through a CVS parking lot, then takes off down another street. Javi tries to keep up. He scrapes over a curb when we make a turn, throwing all of us in the back on top of each other.

"Shit, Javi, you made me spill the Jack!" Cucaracha moans. Javi just throws his foot down on the gas again.

We catch up after about a block, and this kid in the back of the Caddy drops his pants and presses his ass up against the glass. That sets Javi off again.

The Caddy swings into a big empty lot by this run-down park. Javi plows through the patchy grass and dirt to the other side. Before he even stops, the rest of us grab our shit.

"Let's school these fuckers!" Eddie calls as we pile out.

"Hell, yeah!" I shout, swinging a chain. On the other side of the park, a big Chevy Tahoe pulls up with more of the Crazy Crew kiddies.

Now that I'm outside and I can move, I'm feeling good, strong. We roll in a kind of whacked dance, pushing across the field toward them, throwing our signs up. Our blue and white is on our tats, and maybe on our undershirts and rags. Eddie and a few of the boys are wearing blue and silver jerseys. But these fools are decked out like it's dirty Valentine's Day, brown and red popping out everywhere—shoelaces, pants, hats, sunglasses, even. Pinche posers.

They walk toward us looking cocky since they've got us outnumbered. But these are soft midtown boys. We'll whip them fast.

We start throwing our bricks and chains at them. They dodge and shout shit. Their guys have pipes, but I can tell they don't know how to fight. Babies. They'll be running scared soon.

Chuy hits this tall, fat dude with a brick. I start smacking another guy's legs with the chain. He yelps and runs without even throwing a punch.

We keep pushing toward them, pitching our stuff, then going after it again.

I'm smacking around this one dude when I see a light-skinned punk going hard-core after my brother Eddie. Eddie's older than me, but I'm stronger, so I go bail him out.

"Chinga con mi hermano, *and you mess with me!" I say. I block the dude's blows and whip the chain around his legs. He crashes to the ground.*

Eddie kicks him in the gut and slaps my hand. "La Mara Salvatrucha controla!" *he shouts. He spits on the fool lying there, whimpering like a puppy.*

Eddie goes after another punk, and I look around. There's a bat lying in the grass not far off. I jog over to it, feeling like a fucking king now that the fight is rolling. I'm reaching for the bat when I see something red flash out of the corner of my eye. I look, but there's nothing. A second later, I think I see it again. I shake my head in case something ain't right in there. I turn quick and catch sight of the red again. And then—

CHAPTER 2: NOW

I dozed off, I guess, because when I wake up, I find some nasty-looking slop on a plastic tray. It's on this ledge attached to the cell bars. I go after it like a madman. I don't care how bad it tastes; it's food. Last time I ate was yesterday morning. Pelón's sister Maribel and me finished off a whole box of Honey Grahams and the last of the milk. Her mom was so pissed she chased us both out of the house. That's how come I ended up rolling with my homeboys when I should've laid low and gone to Becca's. I could've been doing her fine ass instead of getting myself picked up over a fight with some kiddie gang.

I wonder about my homies, Eddie most of all. *Pinche carnalote.* I press myself up against the bars of my cell and stare down the hall to see if maybe he's here somewhere. If he is, I can't tell. From what I can see, most of the fools in here are still hunched up under their blankets, and it's quiet as hell. I look out at the cell across the way. Somebody's in there, but he ain't moved off his bed once while I've been awake.

"Hey! Hey, *cabrón!*" I call to him. "What you gonna do, sleep the whole day?"

The body in the bed shifts a little, but the dude doesn't say anything.

"I'm talking to you, man. Help me out here. Where the guards at?"

I keep at it until finally the guy in the other cell lifts his head up. He's a skinny kid who looks part black, part Hispanic, maybe a little Vietnamese or something. Like maybe he's a baby Tiger Woods.

"Hey, Tigs, you gonna answer me or what? You seen another guy? Like me, only taller and kind of fat and not so good-looking?"

Baby Tiger shoots me the finger and lays back down on his cot. I guess I'll have to find out about Eddie on my own.

There's something messed up here. I mean more messed up than your usual lockup. I haven't seen a single guard walk the hall yet. And the quiet. Prison is a noisy place; dudes all the time yelling insults and adding crazy ice to their stories about what they did to get put away. The quiet here crowds in on me, makes it hard to think.

I keep trying, but I can't remember nothing else about what happened. I just see the same stupid scenes, sometimes with a voice-over of what I know Becca would say. Things like, "Javi's stepsister *is* a ho; how you going to go start a fight for someone speaking the truth?" and "Azzie, get your ass out of that van!" and "You ain't *nunca* gonna feel ready to change, Azael. You just got to do it."

Then I'm seeing the red, just a flash of it, and that's it. Yeah, so yesterday I was a little messed up from hitting the bottle and the blunt in the car and tossing pills before that. But I ain't never blanked out like this. The memory's there; it's got to be. I just have to find it.

Plus I got to keep myself awake because I don't want to miss it if somebody comes to bring more food. I've got some questions I want to ask. Maybe they just picked me up because I'm brown and some racist cop decided I was an illegal. Well, I'm not. I'm as American as him or anybody else. But I'm *salvadoreño*, too, because that's in my blood.

"Be at peace, Ma," I say out loud. When I think of El Salvador, I think of her. Maybe it's because I've never seen my country for real, never even left Texas except to go to Cali once, but in my mind, my mom and El Salvador are kind of the same thing. That's why the tat on my neck says *Perdóname madre mía* over the flag of El Salvador. Because *la vida loca* takes you places no mother would want to see.

Sometimes before a rumble I cross myself like Ma taught me when I was little, and I hold my fist against my chest. That's where I've got the tat that's just for her. It's a big barbed-wire heart around a rose. Underneath it says *Descansa en paz* and my ma's name, Rosa.

I can almost hear this song she used to sing to Eddie and me so we'd go to sleep, and I know she's close. But I can't remember what she looked like. I remember her hands, but I can never see her face. When I try, it's like looking at a reflection in those cheap-ass metal plates they put up in park bathrooms instead of mirrors. I know what should be there; I know I'm looking for my ma, but what ought to be her face is just a bunch of blurred shapes.

CHAPTER 3: THEN

Me and Eddie were coming home from Pelón's apartment when we saw cruisers outside our unit at the Bel-Lindo.

"*La placa* come to deport somebody's grandma," Eddie said, kicking a spray of gravel toward the cop cars.

"Come on, *huevón!*" I gave Eddie a shove. "If Pops ain't home, we can finish off his beers. Race you!" I took off running.

"Cheater!" he shouted, but there was no way he'd win anyway.

Eddie was older than me by a year and a half, but I was smarter by three. He'd only just dropped out and clicked in with MS-13 even though at sixteen he still wasn't done with ninth grade. School was a waste for us; I figured that out by the end of seventh grade. Better to work and send money out to our kid sister Regina in California. At least that way we was halfway good to somebody.

I was almost up the first flight of stairs when I heard Pops talking. I threw my arm back to stop fat-ass Eddie as he came up breathing hard behind me.

"What?" he asked, all stupid.

"*Cállate*, man. The *pinche migra* is right there."

I looked up through the railing and tried to sort out all the I.C.E. flak jackets. Maybe that drunk-driving rap had to catch up to Pops sometime, but it wasn't like immigration had nobody worse to mess with. Child molesters all running free.

"But what about my kids?" Pops was saying. "I got three, all U.S. citizens. Their ma, she's . . . I'm all they got."

"Child Protective Services will take care of them if there are no willing relatives." The cuffs clicked around our dad's wrists.

"Shit!" Eddie said. "I ain't just standing here while they do that!"

"Shut up and think, *cabrón*," I said, dragging him back down the steps and around to the side of the building. "We go over there, they're going to have our asses separated into foster shitholes, get it? We got to stay clear for now."

A second later the agents came down the stairs. We watched from the shadows as they pushed our pops into a cruiser. He didn't fight.

Eddie shook his head and kicked the side of somebody's busted-up Honda. He looked damn blubbery for a guy with a broken nose and a new tattoo blistering across his back. Our crew called him Etcher, but he'd always be fat-ass Eddie to me. Finally he pulled himself together. "*Pinche pendejos.* Guess it's a good thing Regina's in Cali with Abue. What are we gonna do? Hitch out there?"

"No way I want to spend my nights watching *telenovelas* with Grams," I said.

"Think we should call Beto and Roxann?"

"Hell, no. Tío Beto hates my ass."

"*Entonces, ¿qué?* Can't stay in the apartment. They'll find us for sure. And without Pops we ain't got the *plata* to pay for it anyway."

"We'll get our shit and clear out, then. This is our hood, we know our way around. CPS ain't going to care that much what happens to us."

We waited till the cruisers pulled out, then we ran back up the stairs, loaded up what we could carry, and hit the streets.

CHAPTER 4: NOW

An ugly dream kicks me awake. I lie on my cot with sweat beaded up on my forehead and my mind full up with this image of Eddie's face, then somebody's hands covered in blood. Just a dream. Eddie's fine. Probably he's at Pelón's eating a peanut butter sandwich, getting high, and scratching his fat butt. Nothing to worry about.

The light's still on in the main hall, but everything is dead. I can see a couple other fools in cells across the way, most of them sleeping. That's what I've been doing most of the time, too. Seems like the number one occupation around here.

I've got no idea just how much time is passing. I try to judge by how hungry I feel, but I'm always hungry. Becca's the only girl I've ever met who didn't freak out at how crazy I get over food. She just laughs and brings me back into the kitchen and dishes out some of her ma's soup or reheats a *pupusa* for me. She's cool about it. "*Come bien*, baby," she said one time. "Eat up. You just got an appetite for life." It was so damn sweet I wanted to throw her down and get freaky right there on the kitchen floor. Start working on making a dozen *Azaelitos* with her. Me and her and the *bichos* would roll in a tricked-out Hummer and we'd have a fine house with two bathrooms and a yard and everything.

Before Becca, I never wanted to stick with any one female. I love my homegirls, and nobody better mess with them. But I also know them like I know my streets, and everything about them is rough. How they talk, how they move, how they say your name, how they want to have sex. When we're hanging, they punch me in the arm and say, "*Pinche cabrón!*" after a dirty joke. When we're doing it, they grab me around my neck and scream, "*Sí, dámelo!*" when they come. I'm pretty sure they copy that shit from some Carmen Luvana porn.

My first lay was this older *heina*, Denise. Denise was seventeen and me just thirteen, but I wasn't complaining. She taught me what was up. "Look," she said, "you gotta learn how to touch girls. Do what they like, and then they'll come crawling to you for more." She showed me how to use my hands a lot of different ways.

Denise might've been a *ruca*, but she knew her shit. I used the moves she taught me, and the girls came back to me like puppies even if I treated them bad. But after we did it a few times, it'd get old. "Screw it," I'd tell the girl, "I cain't be tied down." And that was it. If somebody asked me about the female, I'd just say, "Yeah, *me la di*." I gave it to her, and then we were done. There was always more *heinas*; which one didn't matter. I didn't feel nothing anywhere except my gun.

Until I met Becca. Becca's strong. She's got this way about her that pulls you in like a magnet and this goodness inside her that holds you there. But that doesn't mean she's some innocent schoolgirl. Sex with my Becca is the closest a sinner like me can get to heaven.

Now I close my eyes and imagine her body like a prayer that can get me out of here.

• • •

I'm lying on the cot with my eyes still closed when I hear someone slide open the little metal door they use to pass meals into the cell.

I count to three, then I jump up, thinking I'm going to scare the guard. But this weird old cracker in a white uniform just stands there with a meal cart watching me through the bars like he's not surprised at all. He's got these crazy blue eyes in a pasty face crisscrossed with about a million lines. His hands shake a little, but his eyes stay on me. You don't see that many old white guys working in the tank. This guy looks like he belongs in the pity post at the front of Walmart, greeting the grannies and handing out stickers to kids.

I read the plastic name strip pinned to his uniform. Gabe, it says.

"Hey, Gabe, what's the story? Why am I in here?"

He ignores me and pulls a meal tray out of his cart. His hands tremble so much getting my juice out that I figure I won't even need to shake it.

I try again. "Listen, you got my brother in here, too? Name's Eddie. Eduardo Arevalo."

His expression goes kind of funny, and he shakes his head.

"They gotta charge me with something to keep me here, right? And where's the court-appointed fool they got to give me?"

Gabe points to the empty plastic tray on the floor and motions for me to pass it to him. He slides me the new one with a gray burger, a pile of something orange, some green Jell-O, and the juice carton. For a second, I almost get distracted by the food, but then I lock eyes with him.

"Is there something you want to discuss, son?" he says finally. His voice is pretty smooth for an old guy. Especially a guard. All the ones I ran up against in juvie sounded like they'd been smoking three packs a day since the day their mamas squeezed them out.

"Hell, yeah. I wanna talk about what day of the week it is and when I got here and what the hell happened and where my brother's at. And don't I get a phone call?"

He nods, then shakes his head.

"So what's the deal?" I ask.

"I can send for your case worker. If you want to talk."

"Case worker? Like a lawyer?"

Gabe shrugs.

"Okay, what the hell. Sign me up. How long I been in here?"

He ignores my question. "You need another blanket?"

"Screw that. What about my phone call?"

"That's enough, son," he says.

I holler after him, but he just pushes his cart on to the next cell. I look up and see Baby Tigs is laughing a little and shaking his head.

"Got a fuckin' staring problem?" I say, but really, I don't mind. He looks like he's all right.

CHAPTER 5: NOW

I know it's another day because Gabe brought breakfast a while ago. Now I'm drawing a picture in my mind, a big black truck with Becca sitting on the hood all sexy in a tiny blue bikini with rhinestones that I make sparkle. The clouds in the background spell out MS-13, but real subtle. It's force of habit, I guess, to represent even though I'm trying to go straight. *La Mara* has been good to me in a lot of ways. The truth is that my boys are my family. Becca hates it when I say that. "It's no good if it puts you in front of bullets or behind bars," she says. "Let me be your *familia*, Azz."

Maybe she's right, but it's hard to break away. I mean, I got gang tattoos. *MS* on my right shoulder, *13* on the left. Plus my whole back is covered with our sign, pointer and pinky fingers up and out, middle and ring fingers folded under the thumb. At the pool once somebody told me that it's almost the same as for the UT Longhorns, and I thought, shit, even colleges got signs! But I was kind of embarrassed, too, that I didn't know that. Anyway, even going clean, I don't ever want to get my tattoos took off. They're part of me, always will be.

I'm thinking all this when I hear footsteps in the hall, and I know they're not Gabe's because they're heavier and the shoes are different. I get up and make my bed real fast like Pelón's mom is going to come in and chew me out or something.

I'm guessing the man who stops in front of my cell is the case worker. I size him up and decide that he could beat my ass if we fought right now, but if he had to run a block or two first, I could pound his. Not that I'm going to try anything; that's just what I think when I first see anybody under 50.

He looks sort of Hispanic, and he kind of reminds me of a younger version of my Tío Beto, which is no compliment because Beto is a real *cerote*. This guy has a white uniform like Gabe's, but his belly goes way out. His bottom shirt buttons look ready to pop.

His eyebrows are thick and meet in the middle like maybe they've got some evil plan. He's also got a big mariachi-style mustache, the kind you see in the lame paintings in Mexican restaurants. His name badge says Pakmin. Maybe he's Indian. Like from India Indian.

"Martín Arevalo?"

"I go by Azael." I don't know why, but I feel like I shouldn't mess with this guy. If his name really is what it says, he's probably got a chip on his shoulder the size of Texas from being teased with Pac-Man jokes his whole life.

"Fine," he says. He nods to somebody down the hall, and then after a buzz and a loud click, he rolls the cell door open. "This way."

Pakmin doesn't cuff me; he just has me walk two steps in front of him. While we move down the center hall, I try to take in the other cells without staring. Lots of fools are sleeping on cots just like mine. A few are sitting or standing, and they look my way, sizing me up. I stick out my chin. It's a greeting or a challenge, depending on how you see things.

Just like at the Youth Village, here we're mostly shades of black, brown, and yellow. I catch sight of one pink-skinned kid just before we turn a corner out of the cell block. Cracker must get his ass beat every time they uncage all these other *cabrones*.

Next we go down a narrower hall with lots of doors. Pakmin opens one, and we go into a little room like the one at Youth Village for talking to your lawyer. We sit down across from each other at the table.

"I'm gonna be getting out of this joint soon, right?" I say.

Pakmin looks up. "You think you're ready, my friend?" I can tell that this is just something he says, his way of talking. Nobody's friends in here.

"Hell, yeah," I say. "This place ain't no pleasure palace."

He frowns, and his forehead wrinkles up.

"No offense," I say real fast. "It's just, I don't rem—" But I think better of telling him about the big-ass hole in my memory. "My brother Eddie, did he get picked up?"

"It's just you," Pakmin says.

That's good news, at least. Eddie wouldn't make it three days in the can.

I watch Pakmin, but his face doesn't give any clues. "So what am I being charged with?"

"You can review your file. There are reasons for your detainment."

"What kind of file?"

He nods and motions me to follow him. Everybody here acts like they're going to have to pay a hundred bucks for every word, that's how hard it is to get anything out of them.

I follow him out another door, and then we're in this big-ass room, something like a gym crossed with a library crossed with a grocery store with nothing but aisles of filing cabinets. No windows, just fluorescent lights.

He points to a round table, and I sit down in one of the plastic chairs. He walks down an aisle. He comes back a couple of minutes later carrying a folder that has my name typed up on the tab. It's pretty thick, and that gives me a little kick of pride.

Pakmin slides the file over to me. "I'll come back for you."

That takes me by surprise, but he's already gone out the door before I can say anything. There must be some top-line surveillance in here or else he'd never leave me alone.

I open the file. The first sheet says "HOUSE AD-MITTANCE FORM Q-51." It's got my basic stats. My birthdate, the hospital where I was born, stuff about my parents, plus a physical description. 5'7", 135 pounds, brown eyes, brown hair. Two birthmarks on left cheek.

There's also a date and time. June 11, 2011, 3:08 P.M. That's the day I went rolling with Javi and the boys. Probably it's the time that I got picked up.

The next sheet lists everything from my backpack. I know I left it in Javi's van, so does that mean that Javi and Eddie and them got taken in? Maybe Pakmin is lying about Eddie not being in custody. That crazy mustache makes him look like a TV bad guy. It's always the Middle Eastern dude with the funny mustache you got to keep an eye on. But for now I decide that Eddie and my homies got away on foot, and I go back to reading.

Items Recovered:
- One gray Adidas backpack, marked on the front and back with tags linked to MS-13.
- Three photographs:
  - one of a young girl, approximately age 8;
  - one of a long-haired Hispanic teen female ("YR Becca Hottie" written on back);
  - one of a group of eight boys, aged

approximately 13–21, labeled "MIS
VATOS" (see enclosure for photocopies).
- One sheet torn from National Geographic
with the caption "sunset in the Sierra Madre
of El Salvador."
- One pair of socks.
- One can of Red Devil Delta Blue spray paint,
half empty.
- Two small aerosol spray caps.
- One large aerosol spray cap.
- White toothbrush.
- Small Colgate toothpaste.
- Earphones and a hand-held music player
marked in black, "AZZ'S SHYT."
- Three unlabeled CDs.
- A hardbound black sketchbook with stylized
letters that spell out "AZZ'S PIECES."
- A stick of Degree deodorant.
- Traces of marijuana found in bag.

It seems kind of sad all written out, like all you got to do is throw away my backpack and nobody'd know I was ever even around. That's why I like to can. I tag and work up pieces to represent, but I also do it so that there's part of me out there for everybody to see. Getting smoked out with my homies and then hitting the street until my cans run out, that's what I call a day.

The downer is that some fool comes along and messes with your work, covering it up with their shit. Or punks from the city buff it. A couple of times they had a whole little army of volunteers out in the hood painting over and scrubbing out our writing like that's some good deed.

When they could be doing something real, like building a park or something.

Sometimes I work out a really fine piece on a wall somewhere, but when I come back a few days later it's like I was never there. The fact is that you got to re-can the whole hood practically every week to keep your presence strong. Now that I'm not out there to tag up whatever I can reach, to turn trains into traveling masterpieces, how long before my name disappears?

This is how it goes when I try to read. My mind just kicks off to other places. I drag it back and start looking the sheet over for something about why they picked me up or if they got anybody else, but the rest of it is in some weird, official writing. Like "reason for admittance: F111Rs2." I know my police codes pretty good, and these are something else.

The next thing in the folder is a statement from my P.O., recommending me for early release from juvie. My parole came with three strings attached: living with my Tío Beto and my Tía Roxann, going to school regular, and staying out of trouble with the police. I feel my face get hot because even with all my "going straight" talk, I didn't keep a single part of the deal.

On the street, you got to live by the law of the streets. Becca's always telling me that that's stupid, because where has it ever gotten me? Where was my street law when the judge handed down my time? Yeah, I want to go clean for her, but she doesn't get how hard it is. Only a homeboy can understand. All of us have suffered bad; that's why we're so united.

I keep going through the file pretty much in order. They've even got some school records from Tinsley Elementary with my fifth grade teacher's writing. She called me "smart but unfocused." She also wrote about a time I ate all the snacks we were supposed to have for a party. Guess I was hungry even then.

I'm still reading along when I feel something thick toward the back of the file. I pull it out. It's my black book. I try to save it for my best work, but it's almost full, just one page left. I was planning to get me a new one as soon as I filled up that last page.

Just then Pakmin comes back through the door.

"Ain't nothing in here about new charges against me," I tell him when he gets to the table. I don't want to mention the parole stuff because maybe I'd incriminate myself. Maybe that's what they're hoping I'll do. I don't know whose side this guy is on, mine or the county's, but I'd put my money on the county.

"Is that so?" he says. I can tell he wants me to give him the file.

"I just barely got started here, man. I dropped out in seventh grade. I ain't a fast reader."

"Five minutes, my friend," he says and then disappears back into the rows of filing cabinets.

While he's gone, I take the sketchbook from my lap and slide it partway into my pants. Earlier Gabe made me change from my street clothes into county issues, the same kind I seen all the other fools in the cells wearing. At least they're blue, the only color I'd want to wear. And baggy as hell, practically made for racking shit.

. . .

I sit on the floor by my cot and stare at my black book for a long time before I open it. I can just hear Becca saying, "Damn, Azz, already doing wrong the minute he ain't looking." So I imagine saying right back, "I'ma make a real pretty picture for you, baby, that's why I need it."

Then I realize what a dumbass I am because I haven't got a marker or pen or nothing. So I just look at my old work. Mostly it's designs to can, drawings of us protecting our turf, shiny pieces tucked into waistbands. There's one that I did after my homeboy Doble passed. It's got a coffin with these two angels lifting him out of it like they're going to take him to heaven. If you look closer, though, you see he's giving the whole world the finger as he goes up. Doble was tight, but he was also a mean motherfucker, and it's only right to remember him how he really was.

Maybe half an hour later, a buzzer goes off, the cells open, and we line up in the long hall. Baby Tigs gives me a look and lifts his hand like he's shooting a basketball, so I guess we must finally be going outside for rec. We file out into a concrete courtyard with a couple of busted hoops. There's a chain link fence separating our courtyard from another one just like it. I catch sight of a few females in darker blue county issues going back into their side of the building through a double door.

"Fools never let us out here at the same time as the chicks," someone behind me says.

I tense up and turn toward the voice, but then I see it's Baby Tiger. "What the hell's up, man?" I ask him. He's smaller than I guessed, probably twelve or thirteen. He's got a gold tooth in front and his nose is broke in the same spot as Eddie's.

"Jason," he says.

"Azael."

"So how'd it go with your case worker?" he asks.

"Don't know. Dude barely said a word."

He nods. "They're like that."

"What you in here for?"

"My guess is they got something on my cousin, but not enough to put him away. Keep having me watch him being questioned and shit."

"For real?" I ask.

"Through a window, not in person. They don't let us see each other. Don't let us see nobody, really."

"Shit, I don't even know what they got on me. Couldn't read very far in my file before they kicked me out." I bang the chain-link fence with the toe of my busted-up Nikes.

"Gabe's pretty cool. Maybe you could hit him up for another look. I heard he helps people out before they go."

"Go where?"

Baby Tigs shrugs. "Wherever they get sent. From what I can tell, nobody stays here too long."

"How long you been in here?"

"A week, I think. But it feels like a lifetime, *sabes*?"

"Are you part Mexican or what?" I ask.

He laughs at that. "Dude, I'm the whole world rolled up into one." And he walks off toward the basketball court.

. . .

I try out Tiger's advice when Gabe comes to my cell with dinner.

"Hey, Gabe. Thing is, I barely even got started looking at my file. Takes me time to puzzle out the writing. When do I go back to the big room?"

"I'll look into it. Don't hold your breath, now," Gabe says.

"And when I go back, can I have some paper and something to write with? I wanna take some notes on my case, you know?" This is a load because I don't even know what my case *is*. Really I just want to get something I can use to draw. But Gabe seems to think this makes sense, as far as I can tell by how his wrinkles move a little on his face. He's done talking for today, and he walks away whistling and pushing the meal cart.

CHAPTER 6: THEN

After Pops got picked up, me and Eddie laid low for a week. When we heard that the CPS people weren't coming by to look for us anymore, we headed back to the Bel-Lindo.

The Bel-Lindo was bad parents and crackheads, dog shit and dirt for lawns, and pissed-off fools everywhere, but it was still home. There were things I liked, too. Like Jorge Ledesma's grandma praying the rosary out on the balcony to beat the heat in summer. Or the soccer games with the little guys on the dirt courtyards between buildings. And nowhere else in Houston could you find Mrs. Guzman selling calling cards and Coronas and spicy-as-fuck Cheetos right out of her living room window.

Even after Pops got sent back to El Salvador, we stuck to the Bel-Lindo. Our old neighbors knew how things was for us—no moms, no pops—and they kept an eye out and told us when an apartment went empty so we'd have a place to crash for a couple of nights.

When people got evicted, they didn't bother cleaning the walls or carpet or nothing before they split. Those empty units could be pretty sick. Used condoms and weird stains and a million cockroaches, some dead, some alive. Torn-up photos, suitcases that didn't zip, broken dishes. All kinds of random shit.

When Eddie forced the door to 17B, he knocked over some trash bags. He gave them a kick, spilling used toilet paper everywhere.

"Nice work, shit-for-brains," I told him. "You check the kitchen."

"Fuckin' Mexicans never flush it," Eddie grumbled. He used his foot to push a Barbie doll head over toward the trash pile, then he headed for the kitchen.

I went into the bathroom to see if there was anything worth keeping. An old, gunked-up bottle of dollar-store pine-scented cleaner was all I found under the sink, and I thought the drawers were empty till I pulled the bottom one all the way out. At the back there was a message in girly writing Sharpied right onto the rough wood.

> I aint doing this cuz you cheated on me. Not cuz you hit me. Its cuz if I dont Im scared I wont ever leave you. The way Ima go, I wont have no way to come crawlin back. I aint gonna have this baby. Where me and him is goin, nothing can hurt us.

I stood up fast, not wanting to think about what I just read. But it was like the girl's message skipped my brain and jumped into my legs, and I started kicking the shit out of that drawer. Every time I kicked it shut, it bounced back open, and finally I just had to shove the drawer back in.

I walked out of the bathroom, and there was Eddie chowing down on some old crackers like nothing bad happened in this shithole. But I didn't want to talk about what I found, neither. So when he tossed me a package of Pop-Tarts, I caught it and opened it up. Some girl and her baby was dead, and here I was, eating her food like it didn't even matter.

When we threw down our blankets, Eddie passed out right off, but I lay there thinking for what seemed like forever. I almost wanted the neighbors to get into it or for somebody to break a bottle in the parking lot, anything. It was too damn quiet, and I was stuck with what I knew about that girl beat up on by her man and thinking she had to offer herself just to get away from him. Finally I went and sat in the bathroom and got out my black book.

Mostly I tagged for MS-13, but when I got my hands on enough cans, I'd work out a real piece, like the one I did to honor my moms on the wooden fence between the Bel-Lindo and the vacant lot. I showed that shit off for two weeks before it got painted out by some punks on a city work crew getting their community service hours. Erased, just like that. Some writers take pictures of their work and show it off that way. Me, all I got to keep was the memory of killing it out there with my cans, the thrill of throwing something up on a wall without getting caught.

I was still thinking about the girl who wrote the message. Thinking about her by drawing. I started by sketching in the shapes. "Bel-Lindo" in big letters across the top. Over the bottom half, trash spilled out of some bags to spell out, AINT SO PRETTY. I drew an X-ray shot of one of the trash bags to show a girl all curled up around herself. And inside her stomach I drew an even smaller figure with the weird alien eyes and big head you see in pictures of unborn babies. I put a speech bubble out from him that said, "Damn! Already fukt!"

After a while, Eddie banged on the door and asked if I had the runs or was I jacking off? That made me laugh. I put away my black book and went out, but I still couldn't sleep. Sometimes you just can't.

CHAPTER 7: NOW

At breakfast, Gabe doesn't say anything about my file, and I decide not to push it. I spend the morning shooting the shit with Tigs, but then Pakmin comes and takes him away. After I've counted the twenty-four ceiling tiles about a million times, Pakmin comes back down the corridor and stops in front of my cell. His mustache is a little uneven, like maybe he trimmed one side and forgot the other. It makes him look funny, but I make sure not to laugh. Don't need more trouble than I already got, especially not in here. So I get busy thinking serious thoughts while Pakmin slides my cell open.

"You'll miss rec for today," he says.

"Hell if I care," I say, but really I'm bummed because when you're shut up inside, even half an hour out in the sun feels damn good.

Pakmin tells me to follow him, and we walk back into the meeting room where he took me yesterday. For a second, I think maybe I'll get to see my file again. But then we go through a different door and down another hall. Pakmin stops at a third door and turns to face me.

"Are you ready to talk about what happened?"

"I was just hanging with my boys."

He shakes his head. "Don't you see? You and I both know that's not true." When I don't say anything, he goes on. "The truth comes out here one way or another. It always does." While he speaks, he strokes the longer side of his mustache, smoothing out the hairs against his skin.

"Look, sir," I say, trying to play him right by bullshitting some respect, "why am I in here? Why am I all isolated? I mean, what's with the meals in the cell?"

"We do the questioning. You do the remembering."

"Here's an idea. Why don't you just tell me why I'm here?"

"We have a program in place for you, my friend," Pakmin says. "The focus will be on observation. The subject won't know that you can see her."

He turns his back to me and unlocks the door in front of us. He stands there holding it open for a couple of seconds before I get my head on straight enough to walk through it like he expects. Because as soon as I hear him say "her," I can't help but think, Becca, Becca. Let it be Becca. But just as fast I realize that that would mean wishing my Becca into lockup, and that's the last thing I want.

Still, it's got to be someone I know. Like how Baby Tigs spends time watching his cousin. They're hoping we'll snitch on somebody, right? I mean, why else would they bother? We don't allow females in our click, but sometimes the homegirls get mixed up in our shit anyway. Plenty of girls hang around looking to catch some action. Sometimes they'll do the driving for a homeboy or make a delivery. Could be one of them got picked up.

Pakmin leads me over to a long rectangular window of thick, tinted glass. When we get closer, I see that it looks into a meeting room like the one he took me to before. There's a girl sitting at the table with her arms crossed tight over her tits, but I don't know her. I mean, I know a lot of girls without really knowing them, chicks from the hood we partied with or ones we picked up when we sneaked into the movies. But I don't recognize her.

She's white for one thing, and I can pretty much count the white people I know on two hands, beginning with this girl who works nights at the Stop 'N Go and ending with the truancy officer who comes poking around the Bel-Lindo.

Anyway, she has dirty blonde hair pulled back into a ponytail and big, brown eyes. Maybe it ain't fair, but I decide she's probably been around the block a few times. At least she has the body for it. Nice and thick, tits and thighs sort of straining against the fabric of her navy county issues. Her mouth has got this sort of permanent pout. The lips are classic Angelina Jolie, full and puffy.

I'm planning out what moves I'd make if there wasn't this glass between us when I realize that Pakmin has been talking this whole time. I need to get my brain back on business. Who the hell is she? And what the hell does she have to do with me?

"What'd you say?" I ask Pakmin.

He huffs into his mustache like maybe he's not going to repeat himself.

"Sorry, sir," I say, psyching myself back up into fake respect mode.

"I was saying that the idea behind the observation is that it may remind you of what you've forgotten or failed to share with us. Pay attention, friend. You are not guaranteed these observations; they are a privilege. Maybe something she says will ring a bell. Maybe not. That's your problem."

"Should I—"

He raises a hand to shut me up because at that moment, the door to the meeting room opens. In walks this butch-looking lady, also white. Her hair is short and spiky; she wears a gray polo shirt and khakis; and she has the build of a football player with tits.

"Someone will be back for you later," Pakmin says. He turns and walks out, locking the door to the observation room behind him.

I watch the meeting that's happening on the other side of the glass. I can hear them talking, but not through the window. The sound comes from little black speakers up by the ceiling.

"I'm Janet," the butch lady says, holding her hand out to the girl. "I'll be meeting with you for counseling sessions while you're here."

The girl doesn't move to take Janet's hand, and her look says that she knows this do-gooder routine. I know it, too, from teachers and counselors in middle school who used to sling around that "I'm gonna show that I trust you" crap. Acting all sincere and shit, when they don't know a damn thing about you.

Janet finally pulls her hand back, squares her football-player shoulders, and sets a bright woven bag down on the table. It's the kind of thing that might come from some charity for orphans in Guatemala or from Wal-Mart. No way to tell. Janet sits down and pulls out a file folder, some papers, and a book. The girl leans back in her chair, arms still crossed.

"You answer to Lexi?" Janet asks, looking up from her papers.

"Yeah, when I feel like answering," the girl says.

Janet sits there writing on a notepad. I can tell that the girl is getting bored, and she looks more pissed off than ever. I just stare at her, waiting for some kind of spark. Lexi. I say the name a couple of times. But this girl's got no place in my life.

Finally Lexi busts out with, "Aren't you supposed to counsel me and shit?"

Janet gives her a long look.

"So we're just going to sit here?" Lexi asks.

"I get paid no matter what," Janet says. "All your lawyer cares about is having a piece of paper that says you're in therapy. It's all the same to me. I've got plenty of work I can do while you sit there." She smiles, and her nostrils flare out. The only person I've ever seen with bigger nose holes was my sixth grade English teacher, the last one whose name I can remember. Mrs. Hampton. We used to call her class Hampton Hell.

"Seems kind of fucked up, if you ask me."

"Oh, I'm ready whenever you are." Janet closes her folder, but when Lexi doesn't say anything, Janet goes back to shuffling papers.

Lexi starts fidgeting and making these heavy sighs. Without looking up, Janet tosses the book toward her. It's a paperback, and the cover says *Watership Down*, whatever that means. There's a picture of a rabbit in a field on it. Some cheesecake story.

"I hate reading," Lexi says. There's one thing we have in common.

"Don't read, then." Janet slides over a notepad and a stubby pencil. "Try writing down whatever words first catch your attention when you flip to a page."

Lexi takes the notepad, but instead of opening the book and writing down words, she tears out a piece of paper and starts folding it. After a minute, I realize that she's making a paper fortune-teller like the girls in my elementary school used to.

Janet looks up. "Let me know how that works out for

you," she says, "or if you feel like trying my suggestion." She reaches over and takes back her pencil.

Lexi rolls her eyes and leans back in her chair, but after a couple more minutes of Janet ignoring her, she drops the chair legs back down and grabs the book. "Give me the fuckin' pencil and I'll do your damn game," she says to Janet.

Janet rolls her the pencil.

Lexi flips through the pages of the book for a while; then she starts scratching words onto the notepad.

A little while later Janet closes her folder and looks up. "What've you got?"

"You want me to read the words?"

"Sure," Janet shrugs. "Why not?"

"Fine," Lexi says. "Bridge. Ditch. Fighter. Bite. Luck. Soft. Patrol. Silver. Dog. Lost. Whisper. Burrow. Starch. Jacks. Stumble." Lexi sets the notebook down on the table. "That's it. Oh, except I think I came across 'Fuck you, bitch' on one page. Can't remember which one, though." She gives Janet a fake smile and then laughs.

Janet doesn't react. She just says, "Thanks for sharing your words," and goes back to her papers.

"So?" Lexi says after a minute. "What does it mean?"

"What does what mean?" Janet looks up.

"The words I picked. That's supposed to say something about me, or some shit, right? Isn't that the point?"

"Nah, it was just something to do. But I like how 'whisper burrow' and 'jacks stumble' sound. Hey, time's up."

Janet sticks her hand out to Lexi for another shake. Lexi doesn't budge, so Janet pulls her hand back and walks out the door. A minute later a guard comes and takes Lexi out.

I expect Pakmin to come back for me any minute now that there's nothing left to observe. After what feels like forever, though, there's still no sign of him. I walk toward the other end of the room, which is way longer than I noticed at first. It's empty except for a few plastic chairs like the one I've been sitting in, but there are lots of other windows. The big ones like the one I watched Lexi and Janet through are all dark, I guess because nobody is on the other side of the glass. Saving energy and looking out for the environment even in lockup. But at the end of the observation room, I see a few smaller windows. One of them is lit up, so I walk toward it.

In a second I'm staring into a cell. There's some serious discrimination going on here. Whoever stays here has it a hell of a lot better than me and Tigs back on our block. Instead of bars, they have a plain white door with a rectangle of reinforced glass. The blanket is nicer, and there's even a desk bolted to the wall.

The same guard who picked Lexi up from the meeting room unlocks the door and lets her in. She throws herself onto the bed and says something, but I guess the microphones in her room aren't turned on because nothing comes out of the speakers by the ceiling. I take a crack at this mind control thing to try to get her to change clothes so I can see her tits, but no luck. She lies there picking at her arm, like maybe she has a scab there or something. After a while, she reaches over to the desk and pulls out a spiral notebook and a pen. For a long time she doesn't write anything, just pulls a piece of her hair into her mouth and sucks on it. Then she scribbles in the notebook for a while before she flops onto her side.

I get bored of watching her and keep thinking Pakmin has to come for me soon. I'm looking around the observation room, and I realize that the long wall opposite the one with the windows onto Lexi's side is also covered with mirrored glass panes. Maybe this is how the things look from the other side of the windows I've been looking through, and I'm guessing that Pakmin or somebody like him is probably watching me right now. I kind of have to laugh because now "observation" takes on a whole new meaning. Pakmin is watching me watching her. Waiting to see what the rat watching the rat will do. And maybe there's even another row of windows behind that one, and somebody else is watching Pakmin watch me watch Lexi.

It makes me think of these bottles of drinking water my grams used to buy when she'd visit us. They had a label with a picture of a happy family carrying one of the bottles, which also had a picture of a family carrying a water bottle, and I imagined that that just went on forever. If you thought about it right, it seemed like you'd never run out of water because on every label there was a tiny water bottle with a tinier water bottle on it, all the way until you got to these little fairy-sized drops of water inside containers so small they'd be almost invisible. Or like how when you're standing between two mirrors in just the right way you can see yourself shrinking into infinity.

CHAPTER 8: NOW

I'm cranky and stiff as hell from falling asleep in one of the plastic chairs in the observation room. Gabe is the one who takes me back to my cell, ignoring my questions along the way. He hums something that sounds to me like the *Dora the Explorer* theme song. Regina was crazy about that show when she was little, watched it every chance she got.

Once we're back on the cell block, Gabe passes me my dinner tray before locking me up.

I wolf down my food and stick the tray back in the slot. My cot is a saggy piece of junk, but it feels good to stretch out after sitting for so long. What I need is to figure out who this Lexi is and what she has to do with me. Problem is, my thoughts pinball all over the place, bouncing away from me before I can get them lined up.

Somehow Pakmin and his pals have decided that I know something about this girl. Is that what they want from me—dirt on some cracker bitch? I think up all the chicks who are friends of friends and even the ones who are friends of girlfriends of friends. I try to remember the faces of the white girls in my classes in middle school. I rip through my memory over and over, but I draw nothing but blanks every time. Thing is, even if I was a snitch, I got no idea what they picked her up for. I could make some shit up, but Pakmin's no fool. A pain in *el culo*, but not a fool.

I turn my situation over every which way and start to feel the heat coming up into my face. I'm trapped in a corner no matter how I look at it. Before I can bring myself under control, I'm up kicking the shit out of the cot. It doesn't satisfy, but it's the only thing in the cell with any give to it.

I guess I go on nailing it, because Baby Tigs hollers at me from across the way. "What the hell! You lost the last scrap of your piss-pathetic brain?"

"Screw you," I say, but I stop kicking and throw my arms out through the bars. "You do observation today?" I ask.

"Four hours of staring at my cousin. Boring as hell."

"They put me in watching some female. Don't even know her."

"Fuckin' hell, man," Tiger says. "She got tits and a pussy?"

"Yeah, well, tits." I shoot him a look. "Pussy? How would I know? They didn't let me do an inspection."

Tiger laughs. "What you complaining about? I got to look at my ugly-ass cousin while you got you a chick."

"Bitch doesn't do a damn thing. They left me in there watching her sleep, man, like some old perv."

"Better than the cell. Better than nothing," Tigs says.

"I hear you," I say.

We go quiet for a while. "Hey, Tigs?" I ask. "You think your cousin is a snitch?"

"Nah, I'm the one who knows shit about him."

"You going to talk?"

"Nope, just do my time. They can't hold us here forever." Tigs slaps his hand sideways across the bars of his cell.

"You ever feel like somebody's playing a game with you, messing with your head? Like you know things and then you don't?"

Tiger nods. "Whole place stinks of fuck-up, man," he says.

Later, before lights out, I push my blanket over the side of the cot. With my hand underneath it, I slide my black book out from under the mattress. I get under the blanket and make a tent with my knees so that I can look at my drawings without anybody seeing. I flip back to a drawing I did of Becca right after we first started talking. It's her in these short shorts climbing up the stem of a rose like it was a mountain. Her long brown hair curves over her back, and she's turned just a little so you can see her tits in profile. Damn.

I close my eyes and imagine Becca sitting on top of me, teasing me with her hips like she likes to. I imagine grabbing onto the bottoms of her feet and rubbing the soft center part with my thumbs. She's got these little Cinderella feet that look super sexy in shoes with big-ass heels and even sexier right there in your hands. I imagine her hair falling over my face, tickling my nose. I imagine her whispering, "You go straight for me, Azz?"

I feel my gun down in my pants standing up hard, like it wants to answer her question. Fact: she's not here. I take care of it myself, but it ain't no fun like with Becca.

CHAPTER 9: THEN

I was at a *quinceañera* for Pelón's cousin Tina when I saw Becca for the first time. Pelón was supposed to be making sure nobody stole the beer, but like usual he was off getting high. Promised me a joint for covering for him. So I was standing by the coolers when this girl in a black sequined top and real tight jeans walked into the backyard. First thing I thought was, she's got class. You could see that right off because her *nalgas* wasn't hanging out of some skirt even though she was fine enough to get away with it. Her tits screamed my name, and I had to tear my eyes upward to see what kind of face went with all that sexy. She had these big sad eyes done up real pretty, and her skin looked so soft I could almost feel my thumb sliding down her cheek to her lips. She glanced my way and then walked off real fast toward a group of girls hanging out by the DJ.

The second Pelón dragged his stoned ass back to the coolers, I grabbed a Coke and headed toward her.

"Brought you a drink, pretty lady," I said.

Her cheeks turned red, but she took it from me. "Thanks."

"You got a guy?" I asked.

"Maybe," she said, but I could tell she didn't.

I knew a couple of the girls around her, but nobody stepped up to introduce us. Tina was ragging on the DJ, calling the song he was playing crap. Since it was her party, he switched to *reggaetón*. She went crazy, and all the girls start dancing together like I wasn't even there, but I didn't let it faze me none.

"I'll be back," I shouted over the music.

I came around later with Coronas, and Tina finally introduced me around. "This here's Brenda; she's my girl from the southeast side. These fat hos are Ana, Linda, and Jen. And I know you been looking at Becca all night long." Tina punched me in the gut, but I tensed up first. I got a laugh in while she stood there shaking out her hurt fingers.

When Tina told them my name, she turned to Becca and said, "Listen, girl, don't let the long eyelashes and sweet smile fool you. Azael is trouble."

"Don't worry," Becca said, her voice soft and husky, "I can handle trouble."

And she could. She handled me all night long, dancing sexy and close when the DJ played *bachata*. By the time we went behind the garage and started our own kind of slow dance, I wanted her so bad. Wanted to strip those jeans off of her and get down to business. But Pelón came running after me, saying shit was going down on Bellfort and we had to go.

I put him off long enough to give Becca a real deep kiss to remember me by. She gave me her phone number. "See you soon, sad eyes," I told her.

CHAPTER 10: NOW

I've been in observation for what seems like hours, but there's nothing to see but Lexi sleeping. Mainly it pisses me off that I can't have my black book while I'm in here. But I don't want Pakmin to bust me.

I'm dozing off when a guard unlocks Lexi's cell door and tells her she has a visitor. I figure that visits here will be like at Youth Village, everybody together in a big room that smells like ass with this thick piece of dirty glass separating you from your people, no way to hug them or anything. So I'm already gearing up for another session of bored-off-my-ass while she's gone for her visit. Then I hear voices crackling through the speakers on the other end of the observation room, where the windows that usually show me Lexi and Janet are. Looks like Lexi is something special because she gets private visitation. White-girl privileges.

By the time I get over to the other observation window, Lexi is sitting across from an old lady with permed gray hair and a body that droops under her purple track suit. She's not crying right now, but her eyes are red, and her leathery tan skin looks damp in places, like she barely wiped off her face before coming in.

"Hi, Meemaw," Lexi says. I guess the old lady is her grandma.

"Hi, honey." She reaches across the table to touch Lexi's hand, but the guard in the corner steps forward and reminds her of the no-contact rule. She pulls her hand back like she got slapped, and I feel a little sorry for her, this *Meemaw.*

"You okay, baby? You eating? You sleeping right?" she asks.

"Yeah, just bored," Lexi says. "Why hasn't Shauna been here?"

"We've been talking to the lawyers a bunch. They think it's better for your mom to wait a while before coming to see you since, since—well, you know how it is between you two." She forces a smile.

"I'm gonna be out soon, right? They gotta let me out." Lexi watches her grandma's expression.

The old lady gives her a weak smile but doesn't say anything.

"It's real good to see you," Lexi says, but she can't seem to look at her grandma straight on. I wonder if maybe now she wishes she could go back to her cell and pick her scabs and write stupid shit in her notebook so she wouldn't have to see the hurt in her grandmother's eyes.

"I brought you some Danishes and chocolate chip cookies, but they wouldn't let me bring them in." The grandma stares at her empty hands.

"Too bad," Lexi says. "I bet they'd make me a lot sweeter, huh?"

"Don't you worry about that. And I brought you a Bible. They're supposed to give it to you sometime after the visit. I wrote you something in the back, so be sure to look for it. I'm going to try mailing the yumyums, okay? I know how you love your goodies."

"I'm sorry, Meemaw. I really messed up." Lexi looks down. Maybe she's thinking how she'd like to run around that table and climb into her grandma's lap. Or maybe she's not thinking anything at all.

After a long pause, the grandma catches Lexi's eye. "Baby? Would you let me pray for you?"

Lexi doesn't even look like she's heard, but she nods.

"Okay, then." The grandma closes her eyes and folds her hands. "Dear Lord Jesus, you love us just like we are no matter what things we've done. You came right down into this dirty world to save us, and you ain't a bit afraid of our sins because you already cleaned us of them. We can go from being black like coal to being white as snow if we will let ourselves be washed in your blood."

When she says blood, my heart skips a beat. My mind cuts back to the fight at the park. I remember the dream with Eddie, and I feel sick. Hands slippery with red. I want to believe it's paint. Somebody just stuck their hand in a bag after huffing. But not even my favorite Red Devil Chinese Red has that thickness to it.

So whose hands? Whose blood?

"Lord Jesus, Lexi here loves you in her heart, and I know she can change." The grandma's voice goes all whispery. "Father God, you know that she is a good girl deep down inside. She's got hard times ahead. Take care of her. Please take care of her. In Jesus' name, amen."

She opens her eyes and looks at Lexi. It's a begging look. Then it seems like she looks right at me and shakes her head, only I know she's just catching sight of herself in the mirrored side of the glass. Then the guard tells them they've got two minutes left.

"I love you, Meemaw." Lexi says it fast.

"Love you, too, baby. See you next week." The tears are back in the grandma's eyes, but she leaves before they can fall.

CHAPTER 11: THEN

We went through these huge wooden doors that stretched about a mile up. Right after we stepped onto the carpet, Mami would stick her fingers in the holy water and use it to trace the shape of a cross on our foreheads. The church was like a huge boat, only turned upside down so that when you looked up, you were looking into the bottom guts of the ship. There was a smoky smell that wrapped right up around your nose so you couldn't not smell it.

The colors of all the stained glass windows made my head spin. I wanted to see my favorite, the one with the red heart like a sticker stuck onto the outside of Jesus' body. But Mami was already walking into a pew and pulling us along behind her. Eddie pinched me, and I started to cry. Mami pulled him over to her other side and hushed us both. For a while everything was still. Just the smokiness and the heat of Mami's arm where I had my cheek pressed against it. She smelled like dryer lint and soap, and then I remembered that we were going to have a sister. That was why her stomach was so fat.

Sometimes Papi came, too. Me and Eddie didn't know it yet, but Mami and Papi were both praying for a miracle.

CHAPTER 12: NOW

I've got me a kind of routine. Breakfast, talk with Tiger, rec outside, lunch, observation, dinner, flip through my black book, sleep. Sometimes the order is a little different, like today Pakmin comes for me right after breakfast. But it don't matter. Because as much as I would like to drop-kick Lexi into the next county, I gotta agree with Tiger that something to watch is better than nothing. My expectations are low—a good day is getting to see something besides her just lying on her bed. Sometimes she stays there all day.

But a different window in the observation room is lit up this time. It's about halfway between the one for Lexi's cell and the one for the meeting room. When I walk over, I see Lexi sitting in a circle with maybe twelve other girls. A couple of them are dog-ugly, but most of them are easy enough on the eyes. I think about whipping out my gun when I see this one girl who looks like she could be Becca's older sister, but then I think of Pakmin watching from the set of windows behind me. That kills the mood.

It's the usual group therapy setup, same as what I got put through at the Youth Village. Blackboard screwed to the wall, chairs all in a circle, some hippie fool running the show. This guy's somewhere in his thirties. He has combed brown hair and a face so bland that you forget it every time you stop looking at him. He's spouting the usual counselor crap. Right now he's talking about how everyone has an equal voice in the group. Like just saying that makes it true.

He looks all mellow until Lexi cuts in with, "Then how come you get to make the rules? Or does that mean we can bust up this circle and sit like we want?"

"We're glad to have you with us today, Alexis," is all he says.

Some of the girls roll their eyes, but most of them just sit there.

He pulls a stuffed dolphin out of his briefcase and reminds the girls that they can discuss anything except events related to their cases. But if life lands you in lock-up, doesn't that mean everything is related? And besides, how am I supposed to figure out what they think I should know about Lexi if she never even says why she's in here?

But the leader didn't really mean "anything," because two seconds later he writes the word "disappointment" up on the chalkboard and asks the girls to go around and say what the word makes them think of. "How about starting, Maritza?" he says and passes the stuffed dolphin to the black girl to his left.

Her hair is bleached a coppery color and done up in cornrows. She squeezes the dolphin in her fist like she wants to see its cotton guts dripping out.

"Yeah, sure. It really kills me when there's no OJ at breakfast," Maritza says and tosses it real fast at the next girl without even turning to look at her.

"Bitch," the next girl says catching the dolphin just before it hits her in the face.

"Janela," the leader says in a warning voice that makes me think of kindergarten.

"Pass," Janela says, staring at him.

The girl next to her has her hair cut short, and her tits are smashed flat as a board. She stares daggers at the leader. "Your ugly face disappoints me."

When the dolphin gets to this Vietnamese chick, she pops her gum and shrugs. "How I suppose know what word means?"

A tall, skinny Hispanic girl with her hair combed halfway in front of her face takes the dolphin and slams it down onto the floor. "I hate it when my boyfriend cums and I don't!" She busts out laughing, and a couple of other girls join in.

The leader kind of scrambles to the middle of the circle to pick up the dolphin. "That's enough," he says. "Let's pause here. Remember, group is what you make it."

One girl calls out, "Then let's make it a party and get us some shit to smoke in here."

"I think you know what I mean, Taneesha," he says. "Let's keep going, but focus on experiences that may help us understand ourselves better. Let me give you an example. My dad used to say, 'I'm going to take you fishing.' I'd get all excited and think, it'll be this weekend for sure. I'd get my rod ready and wait. But whenever I asked about it, he'd make up an excuse. The weather, or his back, or he can't borrow the boat, always something. It got to where I knew it wasn't going to happen, but I kept on hoping. And he kept on letting me down. That's what 'disappointment' makes me think of."

He could be a shrink on a talk show; I don't believe that crap about fishing with his dad for a second. Sounds like made-up junk he cribbed from some counselor book. He probably knows as good as everybody else that he's full of bullshit. When he smiles, I see that he's got teeth so bad that I know his mom must've thought DISAP-POINTMENT big time when she saw them coming in all crooked.

"Candezz?" he asks, tossing the dolphin across the room to the girl next to Taneesha.

"My mom ain't showed up even once for a court date. She act like I'm dead instead of her daughter."

"Thank you, Candezz." He nods, and she hands the dolphin over to the next girl. She just stares at a spot on the floor, moving the dolphin from one hand to the other.

Finally she speaks up. "I don't get to see my baby but twice a year. There, you happy? Now I feel like shit."

It goes on like that until they've been around the circle twice. Whenever the dolphin comes to Lexi, all she does is uncross her arms and pass it on.

CHAPTER 13: NOW

I don't know why, but it seems like Lexi hasn't been out of her cell in a couple of days. Just lies there all day long with her notebook, which means that the White Girl Channel has been boring as hell.

Finally today the door to her cell opens and Janet walks in. She sits down in the chair by Lexi's desk.

"You okay?" Janet asks.

"Why wouldn't I be?" Lexi doesn't even sit up; she just stays stretched out on her bed.

"Sad news, about the girl in C-block."

"Didn't know her."

"What do you think about people dying young?" Janet says it easy, like it's a normal thing to wonder.

"Don't matter. You got a game or something for us to do?"

Janet opens her bag and tosses Lexi a container of Play-Doh.

"Bad ass, I haven't played with this since I was like seven," Lexi says. She peels back the lid and drops a green lump into her lap.

Lexi sits there fiddling with the Play-Doh, rolling pieces into long ropes, crisscrossing them, mashing it all back together. Janet pulls out some papers and starts filling out forms on the desk. After a while, she looks at Lexi and asks, "You religious?"

"Hell no. Why?"

Janet points at Lexi's lap. She has the Play-Doh laid out in a crooked cross.

Lexi rolls her eyes, then balls the cross up and squeezes the Play-Doh in her fist. "Better?" she asks.

Janet doesn't say anything, and after a while, Lexi goes back to messing with the Play-Doh. She's making something that looks like devil horns to me, or maybe a moon, but with spikes on the side. Then she mashes that up, too.

"Your lawyer told me about Theo," Janet says finally.

"Yeah, well, Theo didn't do a damn thing."

"But it hurt you to lose him."

"No shit, Sherlock."

"You think you're to blame?" Janet asks.

"I'm in here; how the hell can it be my fault?" she says. But I don't believe her. Because when Lexi says this, she looks at the drain by the toilet. I swear she's wishing she could disappear down it and out of her cell, away from that question.

I'm watching for what will happen next and wondering who this Theo is to Lexi, but Pakmin comes and gets me before I can find out.

· · ·

During rec, me and Baby Tigs chill together, talking shit and doing pushups until our knuckles are bloody with gravel.

"That's killer," Tigs says. He jumps up and wipes his fingers across his county issues, then drops back against the fence and slides down until he's sitting on top of some ratty-ass weeds grown up through the chain links.

"I'm getting nowhere with this ho they got me watching," I say.

"Man, don't start up on that again. Nobody gets nowhere with their obs, far as I can tell."

"What gets me is how they act like we should be figuring shit out. What the hell, you know?" I say, but I can tell Tiger isn't listening. He's got this far-off look on his face.

"Tigs?" I ask.

He looks at me funny. "What?"

"Where'd you go, man? You tripping on something you're not sharing?"

He shakes his head. "Just trying to remember. Always trying to remember."

· · ·

About thirty minutes after he brings lunch, Gabe walks back my way. I shove my black book under the mattress before his footsteps get too close.

I'm already waiting by the bars when he comes up and unlocks my cell.

"What's up?" I ask him.

"You wanted to see your file again," he says.

"That's tight, man, thanks."

I stare at the perfect white of his uniform as I go out of the cell. I can't find a single speck of dust or nothing on it. Shit, when I wear white, every not-white thing in the world flies at me and gets on my clothes. I wonder if maybe Gabe's got a wrinkle-faced old wife to help him keep his things so nice.

Gabe takes me back to the conference room where I talked to Pakmin, then we pass through into the giant reading room. He sits me down at a table and pulls out a few rolled-up sheets of paper and a pencil from his pants pocket. He sets everything in front of me and says, "Wait."

A minute later he comes back with the same folder Pakmin gave me last time.

"I don't know how long I can give you, son," he says. "But when I come back, you have to leave. No extra time."

I shrug and reach for the file. "I'm cool."

I try to read faster than before, but I hear myself saying the words out loud like I'm some little kid in second grade instead of 15. Even if there ain't nobody around to hear me, it's still embarrassing as hell.

I go through the rest of my school files real fast. I skim counselor referrals from fifth grade, shitty test scores, and truancy write-ups from middle school.

Then there are police reports from the times I got picked up for questioning, then the stuff about the auto theft trial that landed me in juvie. I know it's stupid when I've got this whole big-ass file to read, but I start thinking about Pájaro. Everything that happened, it's not in here because I didn't get caught. But I ain't forgot it.

I don't even know what happened to Pájaro's girl, Trippy. She lived with her mom and a little brother, and one night they just disappeared. *Se borraron*. Probably gone back to El Salvador, some people said. I didn't even know until Becca told me on the phone while I was in juvie. I was going to do like Trippy asked, find that Mexican and make him pay for what he done to Pájaro. I even bought a piece off of a guy to do the job. Then the next day they picked me up for grand auto, for something I did almost a year before me and Pájaro stole that damn stereo. After I got out of juvie, I found out that other homies took care of things, sent a real strong message. But I wasn't there. Becca said that was a blessing in disguise because otherwise I might've got killed. The thing with Pájaro still weighs me down real bad, though.

Gabe is probably coming back any second, so I grab the last few pages from my file and sandwich them between the pieces of paper he gave me for notes. I roll it all up again like it was when he handed it to me. I barely have time to stick the pencil in the waistband of my pants before he comes back through the door.

Gabe doesn't search me when he takes me back to my cell, doesn't say a thing about the missing pencil. In the Youth Village they had every sharp numbered; no way of getting out of the GED room with a "weapon" like a pencil. Maybe old Gabe forgot, or maybe he gets that a person needs something to do with the long hours on the inside.

First thing I think about is looking at the papers I took from the file. But then I decide I got to make my reading material last at least a little. I flatten the pages out and hide them under the mattress. The pencil goes there, too. Then I lie down, liking the fact that there's secrets I can keep even in lockup, secrets hid right under my toes.

CHAPTER 14: THEN

I pressed my face against the driver's side window. One glance and I knew this kind of stereo was good, none of that anti-theft crap on it. I stepped back and nodded to Pájaro. He smashed the window with a pipe and opened the door on the driver's side.

"Now yank that shit out," he said.

I pulled the stereo box forward, and Pájaro slashed the wires. He reached over the seat and grabbed a stack of CDs from the back and shoved a handful of change from the cup holder into his pocket. Two seconds later we were flying down the street in Pájaro's mom's Sentra, laughing like hell. It was maybe three months after I got clicked into MS-13, and everything seemed hilarious and badass at the same time.

Pájaro parked in an alley maybe half a mile away, and we took a look at the shit we'd jacked. Six stereos that we could unload easy. But when we started checking out the music from the truck, we had to laugh. "This music is shit, man," Pájaro said. He shoved open his door and got out. I grabbed my bag and followed him, and a second later we were walking down the alley, snapping CDs and stomping the cases as we went.

"Fuckin' Tejano? That *cabrón* was asking to get his stereo jacked," I said. I snapped the last CD, then pulled out a baggie with the pills I scored last night from a homegirl at the Bel-Lindo.

"You brought me candy, huh?" Pájaro asked, grinning. "What kind?" He was already working up a spit so he could swallow them easy.

"Hell if I know. Uppers, so who cares?"

We tossed back the pills, then I pulled out a can and started tagging the wall behind us. Thirty seconds later, "MS-13" popped out in these 3-D block letters I'd been practicing. I zipped AZZ into the curve of the three.

"Not bad, *carnalito*," Pájaro said. He walked over to the wall and sniffed the still-wet paint. I tossed him the whole can, and he sprayed some into the cap and held it up to his nose. "I love smellin' these blue roses!" he said. He started laughing.

I kicked a few of the CD cases. "There was some decent rims on that truck, man. We've got the wrenches. How come we didn't take 'em?"

Pájaro's eyes were already shiny. "'Cause you're a *pinche* moron, *culero*." He punched my shoulder. "And you're going to hell for being so greedy."

"*A huevo, loco,* I'm serious as shit," I said. "I'm going back. Ain't been but five minutes."

"Five minutes is long enough for a pissed-off Tejano-lover to come out and see his truck in *pinche pedazos*," Pájaro said.

"Nah, let's go," I said. I started air-boxing to show him just how down I was, how I was doing right by my crew.

"Fuckin' Azael," he said. But when I headed for the Sentra, Pájaro tossed me the keys and followed me.

We rolled back down the same street with the headlights off, real slow. I parked the Sentra half a block from the truck, and then we walked the rest of the way. As far as we could tell, nobody had even noticed that the window was busted in. There wasn't no lights on or anybody around outside.

"You were right, man; this is cake," Pájaro said when we got back to the truck. He was crouching down, looking at the rims. "The lug nuts ain't even the locking kind." He handed me one of the wrenches. "You get 'em loose. I'm gonna jack up the other side."

I was working on the second wheel when I heard something over my shoulder. I looked back, and there was this big Mexican dude standing behind a tree.

I hit the ground a second before he fired.

"Run!" I shouted to Pájaro. I scrambled up and darted into the street. Pájaro was right behind me when the dude fired again. A bullet whizzed past my face. Then another. He kept firing.

And I heard Pájaro fall.

"Just go," he shouted at me when I turned around. "Get your ass down the street!" There was blood oozing down his leg, and he was dragging it bad when another bullet hit him in the side.

I ran until I got to a gas station and called 911. And then I ran again. My insides were different from seeing what I saw. My insides were different because I was the one who'd wanted to go back.

When I took the car back to Pájaro's house, his girl, Trippy, was there. She ran toward me, crying. "They shooted him so much you can't even tell how he was, how he looked like."

She should have been mad at me, but she wasn't. I should have told her that the bullets that got him were meant for me, but I didn't.

"You get him, okay, Azael? *Quémalo porque* he took my Pájarito from me." Her face was red and puffy, and mascara was running down her cheeks.

"I got love for my homie, Trippy, you know that." I hugged her tight. "I'm sorry, Tripps, I'm so sorry."

She grabbed my arms and locked eyes with me. "Promise you'll get the one who did this."

CHAPTER 15: NOW

When Pakmin drops me off in the observation room, I walk over to the one lit window. Lexi and Janet are in the meeting room. They've already been talking for a while; I can tell by how fast Lexi's foot jiggles. The longer she's been sitting still, the faster it moves.

Janet has her doing something with numbers, and Lexi's doing her best to look bored.

"Any number, one through 27," Janet says.

"27," Lexi answers right off.

"Why?"

"Because that's the biggest you'd let me pick."

"So what would you want 27 of?" Janet asks.

"I don't know. Shit, anything."

"27 knocks upside your head?" Janet plays this straight.

Lexi rolls her eyes. "Don't be stupid. Fine, 27 thousand dollars."

"Okay," Janet says, "how about a number between 500 and 799?"

"603."

"Because?" she asks. People in her line of work always want a because.

"That's Meemaw's address. More my home than any place Shauna ever moved us to."

"You want to talk about that?" Janet asks.

"Nothing to talk about. Shauna's a stupid bitch who can't even keep herself out of trouble. Meemaw's always there for me. She gets me."

"Don't you think that it might be a little unfair to—"

Lexi cuts her off. "You got a piece of gum?" She plays with her hair and stares at Janet.

Janet's jaw tightens for a microsecond before her face relaxes again. That's serious self-control. She pulls out a pack of Trident and tosses Lexi a piece.

"Thanks," she says. She unwraps the gum and sets it in the center of her tongue. "How about we go back to the number game?"

"Sure." Janet flips the pages at the edge of her notepad and then fans through them a second time. "Pick a number from 16 to 73."

"18."

"Really?"

"Hell, yeah. You can buy smokes and lotto cards and shit."

"You ever think about what it would mean if you were already eighteen? Now?"

Lexi snorts. "I'd have slept through a birthday."

Janet gives her a kind of tight-lipped smile, but she doesn't press. "Anything from zero to four."

Lexi stays quiet for a long time with this one, and then she says, "Zero. That's how many memories of my dad I wish I had."

This is a genuine, no-bullshit answer. I almost clap like a *pendejo*; it's that rare for her to give Janet a break. But I can't really judge. I'd probably give my counselor a ball-busting, too. If I had one.

Then all of a sudden Lexi starts talking. "Richard, my dad, he's a real weirdo. He's like almost sixty now, but he met Shauna when she was only twenty-two and still living up in Oklahoma." Lexi pauses for a second, and I wonder why she's trusting Janet so much. But when Lexi bites her lip, uncrosses her arms, and leans forward, I realize that it's not that she trusts Janet. She's just crazy lonely.

"So Richard was in Tulsa on business and liked the way Shauna sang at the blues club where she worked, and wham, bam, a few nights together and she was knocked up with me."

"I bet that was hard for her," Janet says, bland as stale bread because that's how she's supposed to be to get Lexi to talk more.

"He acted like he was going to do right by Shauna, and he moved her and Meemaw down to Texas, over to Baytown. He could afford to do it because he's this big-shot oil guy. He put them up in a little house and came to visit every week. Meemaw says she smelled a rat from the beginning, but it took Shauna almost three years to find him out. I mean, she knew he had a wife and kids, but what she didn't know is that he had two other women set up like her in other parts of Houston." Lexi pulls a piece of hair into her mouth and chews on it for a second before she catches herself. "Shauna says it's impossible because I was too little, but I swear I can remember the last big fight they had. Shauna's eyes got bulgy and her face turned red and she started throwing plates at him, pulling them right out of the cabinet in the kitchen he set up for her. She called him a fucking collector and told him to keep his pussy-hopping dick to himself."

Janet nods, and a tiny smile plays on her lips. "Maybe it's not exactly your own memory, but it's a good story. Was that when you and Shauna started moving?"

"Yeah, except for the two years we lived with Kevin. He was the one boyfriend I really liked. He took us out to the suburbs. That was when I was in second and third grade."

"You say you wish you'd never met your father. Why is that?"

"*Hello*, he was a disgusting freak," Lexi says, but Janet and I both know that there's more.

"Did you ever see him after the fight?"

"A couple of times," she says. "When I was little, every time Shauna made me mad I'd tell her that she was going to get in trouble with my dad. That he would rescue me from her, that kind of shit. So she finally let me go to McDonald's with him just to shut me up."

"And?"

Lexi fidgets. "And that's it. He was a jerk, is all. That was one thing Shauna got straight."

A silence breaks out between them. Finally Lexi adds, "The way he was about kids, something wasn't right."

Janet nods and waits for her to say more, but Lexi's arms are folded again. She's done talking for today. I'm pretty sure she's not done remembering, though, because she has this look in her eyes like she's gone somewhere else.

CHAPTER 16: THEN

The last time I saw my moms was at the hospital the day Regina was born. I was six years old. Eddie was almost eight. Papi had to hold the baby up because Mami's arms weren't strong enough. The blanket on the bed was yellow and covered with fuzz that came off when you pulled at it. Eddie kept grabbing my hand away, but I liked the fuzz so much I didn't care if he called me stupid. I played with the blanket, and Mami started singing real soft, *Duérmete niñito, no llores chiquito.* She was singing for the baby, but I liked it all the same. Then the nurse took Regina away in a little cart, and Mami called me and Eddie to come up closer to her. I had all the blanket fuzz balled up in my hand, but it didn't matter because she just reached out to brush my hair back out of my eyes. Her hand was so light touching my forehead it made me think of a little bird, this gray one with a tiny curved beak we used to see pecking around for bugs in the dirt of the Bel-Lindo parking lot.

"You need *un corte de pelo*," she said real soft, trailing her fingers through my hair. "You, too," she told Eddie.

He was biting his lip to keep from crying, but he swallowed hard and said, "I'll get Mrs. Guzman to cut it, Mami. *Por seguro*."

Papi came over, and he cried, too. He put his hands on the back of our heads and pulled us in close. It felt strange to be pressed against Papi's body because it was always Mami who hugged us. I wanted to pull away and wipe my nose, but I didn't want to make him mad. I also didn't want my fuzz ball to get wet.

And then we were going back down the long hall with Papi. Nobody talked about what was happening because Mami already told us how the doctors said something else was growing inside her, something bad, but that they couldn't fix it without hurting the baby. What she didn't tell us then was that now that Regina was here, it was too late to fix it. Nobody told us that.

Mami lasted two more days. She passed while me and Eddie were at Mrs. Guzman's watching cartoons. Papi was at the hospital when it happened. Mrs. Guzman answered the phone, and after she told us and hugged us for a long time, I asked Eddie if the birds in her hands were what carried her up to heaven when she died, but he just kept staring at the TV like the stupid happy music blasting out was all that mattered.

CHAPTER 17: NOW

I'm headed to observation for the second time today. I got to see Lexi in group this morning, and now I'm watching her and Janet play some game called Scrabble, where you use these little wooden tiles to make words on a playing board. After a while, Lexi dumps her letters back into the bag.

"I suck at this."

Janet checks her watch. "We still have some time," she says.

"I've got a headache," Lexi says and pushes the game board away.

Janet starts clearing the letters off the board. When she's done, she tosses Lexi the bag.

"What am I supposed to do with this?"

Janet shrugs. "Whatever." Like always when Lexi gets like this, Janet pulls out her paperwork and ignores her.

Lexi dumps the tiles back out onto the table and starts flipping them faceup. After a while, Janet sets down her pen and fiddles with the tiles, too. She doesn't say anything, but she pulls letters toward her and spells out words. First S-L-E-E-P, then K-I-T-C-H-E-N, then B-O-O-T.

Lexi mixes up the tiles in front of her and reaches for an S. She's way slower than Janet, playing with each letter before setting it down. She spells S-P-I-T and then squeezes in an R and an I to make it S-P-I-R-I-T. After that, she makes her own name. Next she spells out C-R-A-Z-Y. Then Lexi is pulling the A and the Z down from the first word and adding an A, an E, then an L. She sits staring at the word, at my name.

$$A_1\ Z_{10}\ A_1\ E_1\ L_1$$

So she knows me. She has to. She knows me, but what does she know? Maybe she's the one who's not talking.

"Know what it means?" Janet asks. She doesn't look up from the tiles she's fiddling with.

"No," Lexi says. "What?"

"I don't know. Want me to try to find out?"

"Fine," Lexi says. "Whatever."

This throws me because I realize that even though it's my name, I've got no idea what it means. Never even thought that the name my crew stuck me with might mean something. When my homies started calling me Azael, I took it on like everything else, no questions. Now I think maybe I should have asked just what kind of shit I was painting myself with.

Lexi scoots the letters in my name closer together then spreads them far apart. After a long time, she sweeps them into her hand and drops them back into the bag.

· · ·

I've had enough of Lexi by the time I finally get back to my cell. Too much. I feel like talking to Tiger, but his cell is empty. Pakmin's probably got him glued to a chair watching his cousin. It's some stupid shit they put us through in here.

I'm counting the concrete blocks in the walls when I remember the papers I stole from my file yesterday. I'm such an idiot—who forgets something like that? I listen for Gabe's footsteps, and then when I'm sure nobody's coming, I lift the mattress and slide the pages out from under my black book.

First I set aside the blank pages I was supposed to use for notes. I'm thinking these will be good for some practice drawings because I've only got one page left in my black book, and I've got to save it for something good. Then I pull out the stuff I took from my file. It's only about three pages, and I'm planning to just read them top to bottom. But then I feel a kind of a lump on the last page, and I pull it to the front of the stack. I know right off from the hand-writing that it's from Becca. The butterfly necklace I gave her is bunched up in the corner and covered in tape.

2 My Forever Azael,

Take your stupid necklace back. I'm so mad at
you it's like somebody gave my heart a fucken
hot pepper and then wouldn't give it no milk.
I'm so mad at you for proving my mom right. I'm
so mad at you for all the times you kissed my
stomach and said all that sweet bullshit, that you
was working to change. I'm so mad at you for
giving me the butterfly and promising that this
time it was for real because it wasn't. You lied
about changing. You turned around and went
rolling with your pinche boys toward nothing
but more trouble. Javi stinks of trouble but you
didn't bother to sniff. It's your own fault for
going with him.

I had all these stupid ideas for us. Just like
a girl. I was gonna get my nurse aid certificate
one day and you was gonna get your GED and
maybe some kind of training. We was gonna have
enough for our own apartment, a car, maybe
cable. Not the kind of money you thought of,
you and your SUVs and rims and fancy fucken
kicks. But I was gonna teach you how to be real
happy with what we had, not to want more. You
know how good I could always satisfy you.

This time you gone too far and nothing you
could say can take it back cuz you ain't gonna
be talking to me no more. Like it or not, we're

done. And I don't like it because I wanted you and you wanted me but that aint good enough in this world. I'm making myself crazy with all this shit and I can't do it, I got to stop. Who knows if you'll ever see this. There was times before that they didn't give you your mail or nothing. But this is a thousand times worse. There's no way back to what we had. I can never be yours now. It hurts, baby, it hurts, but that's how it is.

Your once one and only,
Becca

This changes everything. Now I know that things are screwed up real bad. The fucked-up rating of my life is through the fucking roof. Whatever they're saying I did, whatever Becca heard, it was bad enough that she doesn't want nothing more to do with me. It has to be something whacked because Becca's real loyal. She's no run-scared snatch.

And then it hits me. I'm not the one supposed to inform on Lexi; she's the one who's dumping shit on me.

She could've been hanging around the park the day of the battle with Crazy Crew. Maybe she got picked up for something, and then the officers came along offering to ease up the charges in exchange for information. Maybe she didn't want to report on one of her homies, so she decided she'd screw me over instead.

It's got to be that. Lexi is running some kind of racket here. She has to be lying because I didn't do anything. Hardly nothing, except for pounding that punk who messed with Eddie. But I saw him stumble away all hunched over; he couldn't have been too messed up.

So Lexi's faking that she saw me do something. Probably tomorrow I'll start hearing her tell lies about me. Just try it, I want to shout. Just try pinning shit on me, white girl. It'll fly right back into your face, bitch, it will. *Pinche puta*.

The heat of my anger cracks against the icy silence in my heart where I used to hear Becca's voice. I picture those sad eyes of hers, so big and brown you could disappear in them. No way can I believe she could mean that it's over. I never would've done this to her. I swear if I'd got her knocked up, I would've married her and taken care of her forever. She can't mean it. Then I look back down at the words written out in her careful girly handwriting. I see the necklace there. Proof that she's done with me.

It's not that I was lying to her about changing. I just should've done it faster.

I pull the pencil out from under the mattress and grab one of the blank sheets Gabe gave me. I'm going to draw something for Becca to make her see that she's wrong to quit on me.

I start working out a butterfly in gray spirals across the page. I draw Becca in the corner sitting with her face in her hands. I put the butterfly on a leash that goes all the way to the other corner. I draw myself there with my best apology eyes.

I'm feeling good about my work until I take another look at the butterfly. When I see what I did, my hand slips, and I break the tip of the pencil.

There it is, twisted inside the butterfly along with all the spirals: LEXI.

I rip the drawing in half and shove everything back under the mattress. I lie down on top of it, but I can't get her name out of my mind.

CHAPTER 18: THEN

It was maybe ten in the morning, and me and Pelón's older sister Maribel were stretched out right on the kitchen floor, listening to Mega 101 and trying to stay cool. The temperature was already in the high 90s, and the AC was busted again. *Pinche* Bel-Lindo, everything *chafa* and broke. We were going back and forth about the question, could you really ever change your life? I thought maybe, but Maribel said yes, all you had to do was decide. She wanted to get a tattoo of a butterfly on her wrist so that everybody could see that she was changed. Transformed, she said. She wanted it right there so she could take a look at it any time and remind herself, too.

Maribel was the one who gave me the idea for the butterfly necklace. I needed something for Becca's birthday anyway, and Wal-Mart had a couple. I picked the shiniest one. It was silver with little diamonds at the corners of the wings and all along the center. When the lady who opened the display case went to help somebody else, I palmed the butterfly necklace and slipped a cheap-o piece from one of the racks into its place. I was out the door before anybody noticed what was up. Anyway, I was changing for Becca, for myself even, but not for Wal-Mart.

I couldn't wait to give it to her. Even though Becca's birthday wasn't for another week, I went to find her at the mall. She was working in this shoe store, and I grabbed her hand and took her over to one of those little angled mirrors that make it easy to see how your shoes look even when you're standing up. I made her sit down on the floor in front of it, and I told her to close her eyes.

"Don't boss me, Azz," she said. She acted tough, but she closed her eyes and tilted her chin up like a little girl waiting for a kiss.

I gave her a sweet one with just a flick of tongue, and then I swept that curtain of shiny straight black hair forward over her shoulder so I could fasten the chain around her neck. "Go ahead, *mamita*. Open your eyes," I told her.

She blushed like crazy. "What's this for?" she asked. "How'd you get it?"

I just told her, "Now you gonna be reminded every time you put this on that I'm changing for you, baby. 'Cause you're my world."

She made sure her boss wasn't out in the front of the store, then she kissed me long and hard. After that she kicked me back out into the mall.

"Before I lose my job, Azzie," she said. She was smiling.

CHAPTER 19: NOW

When Gabe comes by this morning, he makes a kind of surprised grunt. I guess he saw that I didn't eat my dinner last night.

"You all right, son?" he calls from the hall.

I don't move. I have the blanket over my head and I'm not planning on doing anything but lie here for the rest of the day.

"You sick?" he tries again. When I still don't say anything, he starts to walk away. A second later he stops. "If you make me come in and check on you, I might have to search your cell, too. For contraband."

Shit, now Gabe's blackmailing me? I make a lot of noise sitting up on the cot so he'll know I heard him. Last thing I need is more trouble.

I guess he's satisfied because he starts walking down the hall. He's humming again, and I could swear I know the song. Screw him, messing with my head.

I make myself get up off the cot. I don't want to think about Becca, but I can't help it. I pull out the papers and sit back against the wall, right under where it says WEL-CUM HOME FOOL.

I'm scared shitless of what I'll find out, but I've got to know what they say I did. What was so bad that even Becca quit on me? I lay out two pages cut from newspapers. At least I guess they're from newspapers. It's that kind of super-thin paper, but one piece is totally blank except for the name of the newspaper and a date, June 16, 2011.

The other page is whacked, too. I can tell it's an article about the rumble in Montrose, but whole chunks are blacked out with a fat marker. I turn the page all different ways, even look at it from the back, but I can't see what the marked-out words say. What I can read is enough to make my stomach flip.

```
NEARTOWN GANG FIGHT TURNS DEADLY

By Ramón M. Navarro

Houston Chronicle Staff

June 12, 2011

████████████████████████████████

in a gang fight yesterday afternoon in the Mon-
trose area.


At this time of year, the neighborhood around
Ervan Chew Park is usually tranquil in the ear-
ly afternoon, with most residents at work or
```

indoors away from the heat and humidity. But gang violence broke the peace yesterday around 2:00 p.m., █████████████████████████████████

███ ███████████ By the end of the afternoon, the park was cordoned off as a crime scene.

Police say that ███████████████████████████ Mara Salvatrucha (also known as MS-13), a gang made up primarily of Salvadoran immigrants. ████████████

███ ███████████████████████████████████ one of the highest-crime areas in all of Houston.

███

█████████ a fight that broke out between eight to ten MS-13 members and fifteen to twenty members of a Montrose-area gang called Crazy Crew. The Los Angeles-based MS-13 has an international reputation for violence, while Crazy Crew is a home-grown gang of mostly Mexican-American members. The gangs are not known to be rivals.

Police say ████████████████████████████████ ██████████ suspect is already in custody. During the night several makeshift shrines popped up on the edges of the crime scene, including candles, gifts, and spray-painted messages ███████████████

██████████ But by this morning, the shrine
had been destroyed, ████████████████████
█████ and the message had been crossed out. Now
there are several spray-painted messages, also
on public sidewalks, that read ████████████
██████████████████ 187 is the police code for
murder, and in gang parlance is considered a
death threat or promise of retaliation.

The family of the victim declined to comment
other than to say that they hope "whoever did
this will be punished."

It don't take a genius to figure out what's going on
here. The paper's dated June 12, the day after they must've
brought me in here. Somebody's dead, and they think I
have something to do with it. Becca must believe it, too,
the way she was talking in that letter.

I can't remember how the rumble ended. Everything
goes to fog in my memory. But I know I'd know if I killed
somebody. I'd be different inside, like after what happened
with Pájaro. I'd know it for sure.

Something real messed up is going on, because they
been holding me here for maybe two weeks, and I ain't
been charged with a damn thing. That's some illegal shit.
But then, everybody knows that the government breaks
whatever rules it wants to. Just because I dropped out
don't mean I'm stupid. I've heard of Guantánamo Bay.

I ought to tell Gabe that they owe me a phone call, but who am I going to call anyway? No way Becca's going to talk to my stupid ass, not after everything in that letter. Tío Beto doesn't want nothing to do with me; he warned me off when I skipped out on him and my *tía*.

And I can't call Pelón or Eddie or Javi because I got to protect them. I don't want to send the cops their way. If what's in the article is even half true, if somebody on the other side got offed, then my boys are probably already getting hit up by these Crazy Crew pussies. Pisses me off to imagine those brown-and-red raggers messing with my homies, disrespecting my hood. "*La Eme Ese controla,*" I say out loud, like that makes any difference.

I didn't kill nobody in that fight. I know I didn't. But still, shit. It can't get worse than getting pinned with murder.

Only then I remember that it can. Eddie. *Pinche huevón*, Eddie. What if they think he did it, and they're trying to get to him through me? Taking their damn time, for sure, but that don't mean it ain't what they're up to. They might have him locked up somewhere else, trying to keep us separated.

I didn't kill nobody, but right now I'm pissed enough that I could. Too pissed to think or draw. Too pissed to lie down. Too pissed to sit still.

I yank the mattress and blanket off the cot and stand the frame up on one end so that the legs are sticking out. I shove it back into the corner, then I pull myself up by the bar between the legs. Down, up, down, up. I've got myself a ghetto-ass private gym.

My muscles burn enough to calm me down until another thought starts to mess with me. What if Eddie's the one who got cut down? What if that's what they're keeping from me because they know once I find out they won't get another damn word from me? I flash back to that dream. Eddie's face, and then those hands with blood on them.

But if this is about Eddie, why the hell do they have me watching Lexi? What does she know?

I keep doing ghetto chin-ups until the muscles in my arms are screaming loud enough to drown out the craziness in my head again. I know one thing for sure: I got to get my hands on that diary of hers.

CHAPTER 20: THEN

Everything changed after Mami died. Her sister, our Tía Julia, came from California and stayed with us for a while. Papi didn't talk hardly at all, and he never looked at Regina. I think he put Tía Julia and the baby in the bedroom on purpose so that he wouldn't have to see Regina. There was food and nobody hit us or nothing, so we were okay then. But at the same time, we weren't. The apartment felt empty, and nothing was funny, not even cartoons. When Eddie and me left for school, Papi would be lying on the couch, faceup, eyes glued to the water stains on the ceiling. Sometimes when we got home, he was still in the same spot. Other times, he sat at the table holding one of Mami's dish towels and studying it like there was a message written on it.

After a couple of months, Tía Julia had to go back to her family. She offered to take Regina for a while, but Papi said no. By then he was heating her bottles and everything, but whenever we were home he had me or Eddie hold her. He went back to work and started paying Mrs. Guzman to watch Regina while we were at school. And so Regina had Mrs. Guzman and she had me and Eddie. But she never had Papi.

One day just before Regina's first birthday, we brought her home from Mrs. Guzman's apartment like usual. It was early afternoon, and Papi should have been at work, but we found him passed out on the living room floor. The smell of booze on him was bad. Me and Eddie didn't say anything, just took Regina into the bedroom and closed the door. A little later, we were playing with her on a blanket when we heard glass breaking in the other room. Eddie tickled Regina to keep her from crying, and we stayed real quiet until the crashing stopped and we heard the front door slam.

"Listen, Eddie," I whispered, "we got to be the moms for Regina."

"We're boys, stupid," he said.

"You know what I mean. Look out for her. Make sure nothing bad happens to her. You know how Papi's been since . . . *pues, no es como antes.*"

"What do you want me to do?" Eddie acted like he was bored, but I knew he was listening.

"*Promete,*" I said, "promise we'll take care of her."

We made that promise before we even saw what Papi did in the living room. He'd gone and smashed up all the picture frames and ripped the pages out of our one photo album. There was nothing left but bent cardboard, shattered glass, and splintered frames. He didn't leave a single picture of our mom behind. It was like he didn't want Regina to ever know what Mami looked like. And that was a shame because you could see what a good person she was just by how she turned her head a little when she smiled.

Eddie and me took turns cleaning up and watching Regina in the other room. "See? I told you," I said.

"Shut up," he said, taking the trash bag from me. But from then on, he listened to me like we was the same age.

CHAPTER 21: NOW

I'm counting on talking things through with Tigs, but he's not outside at rec, and his cell is still empty when Pakmin comes to get me for observation.

"Hey, where's my man at?" I ask, jerking my head toward Baby Tiger's cell and then looking back at Pakmin.

Pakmin stops walking for a second and rests one hand on his belly.

It takes me a minute, but then I remember how Tigs introduced himself. "Where's Jason? He in some kind of trouble?"

"You're all in trouble," Pakmin says. "It was time for him to move on."

"Move on? Where to?"

Pakmin ignores me until we get to the observation room. "Everybody's time runs out sooner or later, don't you see?" he says as he unlocks the door. "Yours will, too."

I know it's a threat, a reminder that I'm not doing what I should be, but I've got nothing to go on.

"Sir?" I say before Pakmin pulls the door shut behind him. He steps back through the doorway, eyeing me. "I want to—" I pause to find the right tone, "I want to do your program and everything, but I'm wondering . . ."

"Yes?"

"Could I maybe get a little more info about her?" I nod to the lit-up meeting room window where Lexi is sitting. While we're watching, she pulls a wad of gum out of her mouth and sticks it under the table.

Pakmin frowns in her direction. "What did you have in mind?"

"I don't know. . . . I see her writing sometimes in this notebook. Maybe that would help. But probably it's nothing, right?" I don't want to seem too eager.

"Interesting thought," Pakmin says before stepping back out. He closes the door, and the lock slides into place.

The speakers crackle on while I'm still staring at the door. When I turn, I expect to see Janet coming into the room where Lexi is waiting. Instead, a guard walks in with this female who's older but also way skinnier and sexier than Janet. She has long wavy black hair and tits about four sizes too big for her tiny waist.

"Hi, peanut," she says to Lexi. "You hanging in there?" Her voice is all birds and rainbows, but she doesn't really look at Lexi. Like she's scared to.

"Yeah, no thanks to you, *Mom*." Lexi says "mom" like it's this huge joke. "Jesus, Shauna. What took you so long?"

"Mr. VanVeldt thought that it would be better if—"

"You didn't want to see your only kid? You forgot me that fast?"

"Lexi—"

"Just like you forgot Theo."

The lady's face goes white, and she stares down at the table. From Lexi's smirk I can tell she's proud of herself.

After a minute, Lexi's mom finally says something. "I will not tolerate that kind of speech. I'm sorry you're here, Lex, but it's not my fault. Your grandma and I have put everything on the line, borrowed from everybody we know just to pay for your lawyers."

"Did I ask you to?"

"Jesus, Lexi, you've got to grow up. This is no picnic for me. We're on the same side."

"Really?" Lexi says. She raises her eyebrows. "It looks to me like we're on opposite sides of this fucking table."

The guard steps forward. "Another outburst like that and you'll be back in your cell."

"No problem," Lexi says, but she stares at the guard. For once I'm on the county's side. Slap that bitch into solitary for disrespecting her ma like that. But no way am I going to risk getting into trouble with Pakmin on her account. I keep my mouth shut, but my hands turn to fists.

"So what's up?" Lexi smiles like this is an innocent question, but anybody can see she's messing with her mom.

"Just try to stay out of trouble. We need a perfect report from your unit supervisor. Perfect."

"Did Theo—where's he buried?"

Lexi's mom hesitates.

"Don't tell me you put it off on someone else! He was family." Lexi glares at her mother.

"Of course I took care of everything. Just about. Meemaw picked out the marker. We buried him on the family land."

"Christ, Shauna, now I'll have to go two hours just to visit him. Awesome."

"Well, we picked a spot under this real big pecan tree. I think he'd have liked it."

"And?" Lexi asks.

"The landlord at the duplex repainted the fence. You can't even tell about . . . It looks just the same as before." Lexi's mom glances up and meets her gaze head-on for the first time.

For about half a second I think that Lexi might apologize for how she talked earlier. You don't treat your moms like that. You just don't. But it's like Lexi catches herself and the chance to do right by her ma disappears.

I'm not saying I'm some kind of saint. When me and Eddie stay with Pelón, I'm not going to lie, we make a real mess of his ma's house. Dirty clothes everywhere, half smoked joints hid under her couch, dishes all over. His moms spends half her time yelling at us. But she helps us out even if we drive her crazy.

One time when I unloaded some cell phones and got a little cash, I went to the grocery store and spent every penny on food. When I came back to Pelón's place and she saw all them shopping bags and realized I bought the stuff just because, she gave me a big hug and called me a *buen hombre*. That made me feel real good.

There's a way you treat moms, and a way you don't. And Lexi's on the side of the don't. But at least I know one more thing about her: some dude she knows named Theo got cut down recently. Maybe even in the rumble. Somebody died that day; that's the only way any of this makes sense. Maybe it's her brother? I've heard the name, but where? From Janet? Lexi's been keeping her mouth shut, and tight.

Theo, I tell myself, Theo. Need to keep that name in my head.

CHAPTER 22: THEN

When Regina was little, me and Eddie watched out for her just like we promised we would. We had our ways of getting things done. Like dinner was the same every night. Eddie made the bologna sandwiches while I did the PB&Js. Regina put down the plates and got out the glasses for the milk. That was how it always was, even when our pops didn't come out of the bedroom to tell us what to do. For a couple of middle-school kids, we were doing an alright job.

That night the three of us sat down at the little square table, Regina with two phone books to boost her four-year-old self up to the table. She played around with her sandwich for a while, then set it down and put her eyes on me. "How come Papi won't hardly look at me?"

I could tell that she'd been thinking about it for a while. I glanced at Eddie.

"You can explain it better," he said.

And I was about to tell her, real gentle, about how much it hurt Pops to lose our ma, but then he came up behind us from the hall. I didn't see him at first because of where he was standing, but I smelled him right off. The stink of stale cigarette smoke, old-man body, and booze. Saturdays were the worst because he didn't work.

"Wanna know?" he slurred. "You look too damn much like your ma, *lo entendés vos*? Now shut up and eat your sandwich."

Regina started to whimper. Pops took one look at her, then he grabbed her plate and threw it on the floor. Lunch meat flapped against the linoleum, and the plastic dish bounced once. The front door slammed.

Regina cried real hard after that. We did our best to make her feel better, but what my dad said was something uglier than any little kid should ever have to hear. That night me and Eddie called our *abuela* in Los Angeles and then our Tía Julia. It took us two weeks, but finally we worked it out for our aunt to come on the bus to get Regina. Papi went on a long drunk afterward, but he didn't fight it. Maybe we should have done it a lot sooner. And maybe we should have saved up and gone to California, too. But we didn't.

CHAPTER 23: NOW

I think Pakmin likes messing with me because he's got me stuck in the observation room with nothing to observe. I close my eyes, but for once I can't even get into a nap. I count the chairs scattered around the long observation room. Thirteen. Most people would say that's unlucky, but for me it's a damn good number. Maybe something good will happen today. Probably not.

Finally the light comes on in the group-therapy room, and I've got something to look at. There's Lexi's lame ass in one of the chairs. I check for my Becca look-alike, but she's not in the circle today. Another person gone, like Tigs? Or maybe she just had a court date or something.

The group leader writes "out of place" up on the board. I guess he figured out that big words get him nowhere because he doesn't write "anxiety" or some other complicated shit.

He's still annoying as hell, but seeing the girls is a bonus. They take my mind off of Lexi and her stupid snitch self.

This girl named Melissa with soft brown hair tells about how it was before she had her baby. "The judge said I had to go to parenting class. This was before I got locked up. Only because I was living out in the suburbs with my boyfriend's parents, I had to go to this place where everybody else was white and old, like at least twenty-two. I had to sit there with my big brown belly sticking out from under my tank top while they looked at me like I just took a shit on the floor. Like I was nothing."

The leader nods and makes some sympathetic noises. "Sounds like you're still feeling some anger from that experience."

The Vietnamese girl takes the dolphin from Melissa. "She got right to feel mad, I think."

"Hell, yeah, she does." A black girl I remember from the last time snaps her fingers to get the other girl to toss her the dolphin.

"Taneesha?" the leader says once she catches it.

"I can't get over this time when my whole family was going to go to Six Flags. I helped get my cousins ready and everything and we was walking out the door when my mom pulled me back and told me I couldn't go, that my Aunt Jasmine thought I'd be a bad influence because I'd been in juvie. I wanted to fight with my mom over it, but that'd just have proved my aunt right. So I stood there on the porch and watched them drive away. What hurt the most was that my mom didn't stand up for me or nothing. She went without me."

The leader goes around the circle like before. I wait for Lexi to say something, anything that might give me a clue, but like always, she keeps her arms crossed and her mouth shut.

. . .

Everything hits home again when I'm back in my cell. I've read Becca's letter so many times I think I've got it memorized. I try to stop myself from looking at it because it doesn't help things none, but I keep pulling it out anyway. Every time it takes more and more chin-ups and sit-ups and push-ups to get her words out of my head.

It cuts me deep because Becca was the only one who told me to do things or talked to me straight for my own good. I never thought she'd get fed up with me so fast. But she ain't lying, neither. I promised all kinds of shit to her. With her it was easy to dream of things being different, to imagine going straight. I could even pretend myself into the future. Like me being the badass who hangs out with the little guys at the YMCA and tells them how things really go down and what they got to do to live clean.

I always thought I'd be a real good dad, not like my pops, always coming after us with a belt. Not like my Tío Beto, neither. Becca said I hated Beto just because he was making me go to school after juvie. But that wasn't it. My *tío* decided a long time ago that I was bad. He wouldn't let me forget it for five minutes. Sometimes I'd be talking to Becca real quiet on the phone, thinking he couldn't hear me. Telling her about my dreams. Then I'd hang up and he'd walk by and say some shit like, "Hummers don't fall out of the sky, Martín. You'd better start thinking about your future."

Beto wouldn't call me Azael. That really pissed me off. He said, "I stood next to your mother's bed when she named you Martín. No way am I going to call you by some street *apodo*."

Right now, Beto is probably laughing with Tía Roxann, saying, "*¿Qué dije?* I told you he was going to get back into that shit."

I hate it that Beto was right, and I want to do something to get him out of my head. I think about drawing, but then I remember the busted pencil. I pull it out anyway. First I just pick at the splintered wood, then I start scraping it against the sharpest edge of the cot. I get a little chunk of wood off with each scrape. It's going to take me a long time to get a point again this way, but time is one thing I've got plenty of.

CHAPTER 24: THEN

I'd been out of the Youth Village for maybe three weeks. I was doing good every day, dragging my ass to Pasadena High like a *pinche* schoolboy. But this one morning I just needed a vacation from my new straight-edge life. Just one day off.

I was up to my balls in sleep when Beto busted into the room that he let me and Eddie use. When I opened my eyes, I saw a vein popping out of his forehead. He was shouting, "Huevón! *Levantate, vos!*"

He yanked the covers back with one hand and pulled open the curtains with the other.

"C'mon, don't," I mumbled. I crossed my arms over my eyes against the bright light.

"Get your goddamn ass out of bed," Beto yelled. "Ass out *now*. I didn't sign you out of juvie, didn't bring you into my own home for you to start this shit back up again. *¿Escuchá, vos?*"

"I hear you, I hear you," I said. "I'm sick, man, cut me some slack."

"You wasn't sick when you went out last night. Now get up."

I was going to get up and go like he told me to, but he just kept ragging on me, saying I was going to land back in juvie, saying my ma would be ashamed, calling me a bad influence on Eddie.

"Fuck it, man! I don't need this shit." The words sailed out of my mouth. Once they were out, I couldn't reel them back in.

"You want to repeat that?" Beto growled at me.

"I said, fuck it. I'm fuckin' out of here." And then I was throwing my shit in my backpack. Just like that, I quit him, and I quit school again. I quit the Reform Azael Program and caught the 40 bus back to Pelón's house where I could be halfway in peace. A week later, Eddie showed up, too, and we were back with our crew.

CHAPTER 25: NOW

With Tigs gone, I've got even more time to kill when I'm stuck in the cell. I think about sketching something out in my black book. I've got a point back on my pencil, but then I remember what happened before, Lexi sneaking in through my pencil. No way I'm going to let her screw up the last page in my book.

Instead, I burn up some hours planning what I'd do with these cell walls if they'd give me some cans. Maybe what I'd paint is a kind of map of my life, different times laid out like neighborhoods. This is what life looks like with my moms around: lots of green, a park where they give away cinnamon *pastelitos* and balloons to little kids. There's me and Eddie and Mami standing by a fountain that really works. There's Pops walking to work with a lunch sack and a clean uniform. This is what life looks like after my moms died: dark colors, the Bel-Lindo buildings leaning all crazy like they're going to fall down, broken balconies hanging loose. Eddie and me are sitting in a courtyard, circled around baby Regina. She's the one bright spot with her pink and yellow dress. Pops is walking away from us carrying a fifth of tequila. I think about what's next—Regina going away, clicking in with MS, Pops getting picked up, meeting Becca. That's a lot of hoods. Already I've got way more than I can fit on these cramped-ass walls.

This happens to me a lot when I'm thinking out a piece. Lots of times I can't find a wall big enough for everything I want to put in. I get caught up in details I want to add, but when you're working with cans, it's the little stuff that's hardest to paint. Even with super-thin caps. But I like the challenge. For me, canning is about a lot more than tagging up a wall. Sure, getting my tag up in a heaven spot gives me a high, and I make it my business to do throw-ups any time I've got a can. But what I really like is working out a good piece. It's this whole process. First you plan your shit out in a black book, then you look for the right wall. After that, you've still got to rack your colors.

If you're underage, you steal your cans because there's all these crazy restrictions on selling aerosols. That's thanks to fools like Pelón huffing paints and getting mommies and daddies in the suburbs all worried about their brats' brain cells. I can walk into any ghetto pawnshop on the Southwest Side and buy a knife without getting asked questions, but Wal-Mart won't sell me a 97-cent can of spray paint.

CHAPTER 26: THEN

Me and Eddie sprawled out on Pelón's bed, his cell phone between us. It must have been a weekend because Pelón said we could talk as long as we wanted, and he only did that when it was free.

We had the phone on speaker, and it was on maybe the fourth or fifth ring.

"Shit," Eddie said, "they're not answering." He reached for the phone like he was going to hang up.

I pushed his hand away. "Just give it a second, man."

We were calling Regina out in California because it was her birthday. A couple of rings later, our grandma answered. After I said hello and she called for Regina, I could hear her saying, "Go on, talk to him, that's your *hermano*." Finally Regina got on the phone.

"Hello?" Her voice was soft, and I could barely hear her over the shouting and laughing in the background.

"Hey, *chiquita! Feliz cumpleaños!*" Eddie said.

"Yeah, how does it feel to be seven?" I asked.

"Abue and Tía Julia made me a cake. With ice cream inside."

"We're gonna send you a present real soon, okay? Just tell us what you want," I said.

"I've already got lots of presents," she said. There was even more noise, and she started laughing. Somebody was singing in the background. "Stop it, Tío!" Regina giggled.

"You still there, Regina?" Eddie asked. "You want more presents, right? Everybody wants more presents."

"No, that's okay. They're calling me now to do the candles. I got to go. Bye."

Then Abue came back on the phone. "She's just excited about her party, *mijo*," she said. "Don't take it wrong." But she knew just as good as we did that Regina didn't really want to talk to us anyway.

After we said good-bye, we just stayed there on the bed for a while, not talking. It was like we both knew that we weren't really part of Regina's life anymore, but we didn't want to say it out loud. I sat there thinking back to how small she was when she came home from the hospital. I could still remember how it felt to hold her, how me and Eddie were scared we might hurt her just by looking at her.

There was this one time me and Eddie had to figure out how to cut her fingernails. At the beginning, Tía Julia did it, but when she went back to her family, it was up to us. We sat there for the longest time staring at the clippers and her perfect little claws that were scratching us up. But it turned out okay because Regina started laughing at the click sound the clippers made when they closed on her nails.

In the old days, we took care of Regina and taught her everything, even how to tie her shoes. And now she didn't even want to talk to us. Maybe I should have been glad that she had a new life away from us so we couldn't mess things up for her. It wasn't like me and Eddie were Boy Scouts. But I couldn't help wishing she missed us just a little.

CHAPTER 27: NOW

I'm sick of trying to get my brain to play that day at the park. The trying keeps taking me places I don't want to go. I feel like giving up on remembering because it's too damn hard, but there's no way I can handle Pakmin right until I know what's behind me. What I did or didn't do. Right now I can't even remember enough to work up a good lie.

Who knows, maybe they even gave us some drug to make us forget so that they can tell us whatever they want. Like the opposite of truth serum.

But I can't think that way. Job #1: remembering. Who's the patron saint of things you forgot? Ma used to sing us some song with the names of saints in it. There's a patron for everything, she said. For TV repairmen and orphans and people with broken hearts, for dogs and cats, for people who sleep on park benches, for lost causes. Me, I'm my own fucking lost cause.

A name finally pops into my head: San Antonio. Ma telling me and Eddie when we lost our remote-control race car, *hacemos una oración a San Antonio*. A prayer to San Antonio for a lost thing.

Close enough. I imagine that my missing memory is a lost thing. I picture it as a cardboard box, the kind you get in first grade to hold your pencils and crayons. The box is in a big room filled with junk, but I know it's in there somewhere. Show me where it is, I think, please show me where it is. Dear San Antonio. Please. Amen. I almost laugh out loud, that's how bad my prayer sucks. But it's been about a million years since I prayed. Shit, it's been a while since I talked to anybody but Gabe and Pakmin. After Tigs disappeared, the only time I say anything is to ask the new arrivals about Eddie.

Maybe I'll try the prayer again, but I don't need nobody looking at me. I spread my blanket out so it hangs from the top of the mattress down to the floor, and then I think small and pull myself under the cot. The concrete floor smells of sour piss and sweat. For a second I'm back on the Southwest Side running down an alley, the high of canning mixing with the fear of getting caught. Then I'm here again, and all I see is the wobbly weave of the blanket. The sounds of the cell block filter in to me. Instead of praying, I end up listening to the shifting of mattresses, the clearing of throats, the bouncing of springs that means somebody's jacking off.

• • •

"Come get your lunch, son," Gabe calls to me. I open my eyes and see his white pants legs and black shoes through the fabric of the blanket. I roll out from under my cot, feeling like an idiot. But Gabe doesn't say anything about me sleeping on the floor, just stands there with his mystery-man smile. It's creepy at first, but almost nice once you get used to it.

Usually Gabe just leaves the food, but if he wants to talk to me, I'd better get my ass up and take advantage. Today he's holding the tray all funny. Instead of holding onto the sides like normal, he has his hand underneath it like a waiter. When I reach over for it, he uses his free hand to pull my right hand to the underside of the tray. "There you go," he says. His eyes lock with mine, and I feel a hard metal coil against my fingers. "Until tomorrow morning," he says.

"Thanks, Gabe," I say. I give him a nod to show him how much I mean it.

Once he's gone and I'm sure the hall is empty, I slide Lexi's notebook out from under the tray. I fire a thank-you in San Antonio's direction just to be on the safe side, but I'm not dumb enough to believe that prayers work this fast. I'm pretty sure this is all Gabe.

Even though I don't feel like eating, I choke down my sloppy joe and the apple so that nothing will seem weird. Then I lie down on the cot, pull the blanket over my head, and start reading. I figure I've got at least an hour before rec.

Get this, Gray Suit says I should keep a journal. First he brought out this sunflowered piece of shit with a yellow ribbon to tie it shut. No way was I gonna touch that. I told him to give it to his grandma or shove it up his ass.

When he came back with this one, I took it just to shut him up. But if I write in here, it's because I want to.

There's nothing else to do anyway. So far my day is eat, shit, and sleep. That and cross my fingers that Meemaw and Shauna will get me out fast.

The thing is, I'm in here, but I don't even know what exactly went down.

See, I like my life a whole lot better if I'm on a little something to soften the edges. My favorites are Xannies. They mess me up good.

One time Cartoon told me that I let him and Slots touch my tits when I was tripping. "Bullshit," I said, "in your dreams." My boys call me a tease, but the truth is that I don't like being touched. That's for reasons I don't feel like writing about. So I thought for sure Cartoon was lying, so I punched him hard in the gut.

Then he leaned over and whispered something about the scar. It's on my left tit, from an open-heart surgery when I was a baby. And I never talk about it. It's something he'd only know about if he'd seen it.

Anyway, me and Cartoon are pretty tight. He calls me before something goes down. Then sometimes he turns around and acts like a pussy. Tells me to beat it, says there's no bitches allowed.

"What about you, faggot?" I say, and play it off. But it hurts me when he says shit like that. Makes me feel like somehow he doesn't really think I'm down. Like I've always got to be proving myself to him, and he's supposed to be my friend.

Meemaw came today, but Shauna still hasn't shown her ugly face. Meemaw says to be patient, but she doesn't know when I'm going to be getting out of here. She asked me if I wanted her to pray with me like she always does when I'm in trouble. I didn't, but I said okay because I know it's what she wanted to hear.

Here's how being in here is like living with Shauna:
#1 – It's only temporary.
#2 – The walls are blank.
#3 – I'm lonely.
#4 – I'm bored.
#5 – There's shit to eat.
#6 – Shauna's not around.

I could add a lot more to this list, but I'm already feeling mega pissed at Shauna. Yeah, so I call my mom by her first name. So it's kind of disrespectful, so what? She hasn't done a whole lot to earn my respect. Some role model. Always telling me to do the right thing, whatever that is, when she can't keep her own life straight. No way I can take her serious.

Like when she says that I need to work on my attitude, I just roll my eyes real big at her and say, "What attitude, Shauna?"

That pisses her off, and she throws the remote down. I just smile and go, "Easy there. Looks like you've got some attitude too."

Sometimes that gets her laughing, and the lecture's over. But lots of times we just fight. Like last week she asked me, did I skip summer school today? Which of course I did, but no way was I going to admit it. I just walked out of the kitchen and headed for my bedroom.

Then she shouted after me about getting the call from the school. Goddamn attendance office.

I fought back fast. "Who you gonna believe? Your own daughter or some goddamn secretary?"

Then she came into my room talking about responsibility. Blah, blah, blah. Her voice goes all whiny when she says this kind of crap. The funniest is when she starts in about trust. It's all total bullshit.

I don't care if she wants to talk about this shit, but she has to be ready to feel it where it hurts. Like when I remind her that she's the one who got fired off of three jobs for coming in drunk. She starts to cry, and her mascara globs up in the wrinkles around her eyes. God, she's pathetic.

I show no mercy, just go in for the kill. I tell her that the mistakes started with her. We'd both be better off if she'd just gotten an abortion. Had me vacuumed out.

But she didn't. So I tell her to stop trying to ruin my life now. Then I grab Theo's leash and he comes running. A second later we're out the door and out of her reach.

I toss down the notebook. Is this a fucking joke? Theo's a damn dog. Shit. The way she was talking about him with her mom before, I had him pegged for some kind of family, a brother or some *primo* at least. So much for that.

I don't get how some people are about dogs, acting like they matter so much. Whenever Pops saw dogs nosing around the trash at the Bel-Lindo, he'd give them a good kick in the ribs. Regina didn't like that, but we just told her those were mean dogs, not like the ones on TV. Me, I can't see how anybody could have a dog unless they was rich. Why waste good food on a mutt? But you see it all the time, especially with white people. It's like they think having a dog makes you a good person. I'm not buying it. Having a dog is just having a dog.

I think about Lexi on the street with her *pinche* dog crapping in the neighbor's bushes and I feel a little better, so I go back to reading.

Here's my day so far. I woke up at the butt crack of dawn because some ho down the hall was screaming bloody murder. I tried to go back to sleep once the guards hauled her ass off. No dice. 5:00 a.m. and awake like a fuckin' farmer.

No lights in the cells till 7:00, so I had two hours to kill. I thought about Cartoon for a while, but that made me sad because I haven't heard a word from him.

I looked around the cell for something that I could mess with, and finally I found these bolts holding the toilet to the floor. I worked on one of them forever and got it twisted out. Then I spent the next hour using it to scratch my name into the wall right below the sink. I did it like Slots showed me one time when I went canning with him:

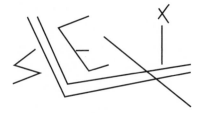

That's what Slots called me. Sexi Lexi. He even canned that onto the back of the Quik Stop when he was tagging it up. Sexi Lexi. Homeboy just wanted to get into my pants. But I still liked it. Slots and Cartoon are tight with each other, but whenever Slots comes around me, Cartoon gets all edgy. That makes it more fun for me. I like them both, but Cartoon's cuter.

It's my fourth day in here. I finally got to go outside for exercise. Hot and sticky as a giant's pussy out there, but at least it wasn't the cell. My little pocket of paradise seriously stinks. Can't even get away from my own farts.

Everything they serve at meals here is in lumps. Brown lump = meat loaf. White lump = potatoes. Green lump = spinach. Puke-colored lump = applesauce. I'm going to die if I have to keep eating powdered eggs and rubbery hamburgers. I want a Snickers bar, Lay's potato chips, tater tots. Chicken strips and French-cut green beans with lots of salt and baked potatoes with butter and cheese and bacon. Chocolate milk with cereal and Meemaw's bakery cinnamon rolls for breakfast. Anything that tastes.

Theo's dead. Theo's dead because of me.

I've been living with it for two days now, but I keep seeing Theo's dopey big head, his tongue all hanging out, the floppy ears. I want to be mad at him. Why didn't you bite them, you stupid mutt? You've seen pit bulls on the block before, you know how it's done. But also I know that Theo was super old and not very smart at all. He needed protection.

I want to push my mom up against a wall and say, "Shauna, you idiot, why didn't you check on him? Why'd you leave him out there to get cut? Why didn't you take him for a normal goddamn walk?"

But most of all I want to kick Gray Suit in the balls for showing me the picture. So what if I said I wanted to see it? He should have known that it would mess me up.

I knew something went down when he came in calling me "Alexis." And sure enough, he goes and tells me that *even though they set bail, my defense team wants me to stay in custody for my safety. I told him right where he could put that shit idea. For my safety?! I'm not fuckin' scared. And I told him so.*

Then he dropped the bomb about "danger to my family," which shut me up fast. I asked him about Meemaw, then Shauna. In that order. I needed to know. I even said "please," trying not to be a bitch about it for once.

Gray Suit pulled out this photograph, held it face-down against his notepad. He looked like he was ready to shit a brick. Then he told me about Theo.

I told him to let me see the picture, that I had to see it. And I swore to myself that I was not gonna cry in front of him.

For a long time he just stared at the Kodak stamp on the back of the picture, didn't say anything. Finally he flipped it over, but he still kept half of it covered with his notepad.

The part that I could see showed the fence behind our duplex. There was a message spray-painted on it in dripping black letters: 187 DIE BITCH 187. I knew that Gray Suit was hiding the part of the picture that had my dog in it because I could see the tip of Theo's tail.

I told him I wanted to see the whole picture.

He asked if I was sure and looked right at me for the first time I can remember.

When he uncovered the whole picture, there was Theo. If I only looked at his face, it was easy to pretend he was just lying in the backyard taking a nap. But then I saw the dark red mess spilling out of him and mixing with dirt. It looked like somebody unzipped his belly. There was a big knife still stuck in him, and I thought I was going to be sick.

Gray Suit's voice seemed far away, and it faded in and out like a radio in a car whose antenna got jacked. Saying shit about the safest thing, about my protection, about a police watch for Meemaw, about the time before the trial.

But none of that matters, because Theo's dead. I know that no matter how I spin it, this one's all on me. I might've done other bad shit that I can't write about here, but Theo didn't do nothing. He was just a dumbass dog with a sweet heart. This one's all on me, and it sucks.

I didn't know that I was crying until just now when I messed up the ink in here with my stupid tears.

If this is how she gets over her dog getting cut up, what would she do if one of the punks in her kiddie gang got offed? Would it be enough to make her lie? To make her pin it on one of us, no matter who did it? She might get a break from her own charges for revealing information, and until I remember something, I can't prove she's lying. But all this takes me back to the question of why she's locked up in the first place. What have they got on her? She's been sticking her fingers in somebody's business if she's getting threats like that thing with her dog.

I need to keep reading, but my eyes are already tired. I take a few turns around my cell, probably looking like a dog in a cage. Then I dive back into the notebook.

Gray Suit just brought me my new schedule. Like he's some kind of school counselor. He's been fighting with the boss of the place over whether I should be eating in the cafeteria with what he calls the youth offenders. The people in charge don't want to give me special treatment. Gray Suit said he made them because I'm being kept here for my protection. He said it isn't safe for me to be around everybody else. They're a threat to me, he said. No way to know until it's too late who's representing who.

I told him I could take care of my own damn self, don't care what gang a bitch is in; she won't mess with me. He looked like he was going to cough up a hairball and said no, the worst thing possible would be for me to get into an altercation with someone here.

So here's the deal:

```
ALEXIS ALLEN SCHEDULE
All programming subject to change and cancellation.
7:00 a.m. - breakfast in unit
9:00 a.m. - supervised group therapy
12:00 p.m. - lunch in unit
1:00 p.m. - supervised recreational time in TV room
```

```
2:00 p.m. - one-on-one therapy
4:00 p.m. - supervised recreational time in gym/
courtyard
6:00 p.m. - dinner in unit
```

There ought to be a Xanax and cookie happy hour where Cartoon comes to visit me. I want him to tell me what him and the boys have been up to. I want to know what they're going to do about Theo.

Gray Suit must have said that I needed someone tough for therapy because they stuck me with some dyke. Janet. She started out all, "this is going to be different, I'm here to help," but as soon as I pushed her buttons a little, you could tell that she didn't want to be there any more than I did.

A lot of things about Shauna piss me off. There's one thing that's worse than the rest, though. My friends think she's hot. How embarrassing is that? One time one of Cartoon's friends wrapped his arm around my shoulder and said, would I mind if he did my mom just once to see what it was like? Pissed me off for a whole day.

Shauna runs around in leggings and little shorts and a shitload of makeup. She even has a stupid sweatshirt with PINK printed across the front just like the skinny girls at my school. Who does she think she is? She chooses not to accept that you can't dress like that when you're forty.

I need out of this place. I'm hungry for a crazy night with my homies, at least with my boy Cartoon. He always makes me laugh and forget what shit life is. And he's always got a good supply of bars.

When I'm just sitting in here, if I close my eyes, I can almost feel a bar of Xanax in my hand. Once I could have sworn I even broke a block off. I was just dying to put it in my mouth and feel the world go soft and me get invincible. But when I opened my eyes I was just holding onto the corner of my notebook.

Today when I got back to my cell after outdoor rec there was a Bible on my bed, the one Meemaw sent for me when she came last, I guess. It was a real nice hardback, but they cut off the front and back covers.

So far I've just held it in my lap and traced the words "Holy Bible" on the first page. She said there was a note in it for me. I'm afraid that if I read what she wrote, I'll start crying again. Since I saw Meemaw, being here seems way too real, and I can't stand it. I wish I could go home and listen to my music and hug Theo and feel him lick my ear and even have a conversation with Shauna that maybe doesn't end in shouting if she doesn't act like such a bitch.

But Theo is dead, and Shauna is a shitty mom who doesn't even care about me.

I opened the Bible to the back and read what Meemaw put there. She said I was a good person with a good heart even though I've been going with the wrong people. She wrote about how when she got pregnant with Shauna at fifteen her aunt helped her out and told her that God cares about everybody. She wrote that He loves us enough to go look for a lost sheep no matter how far it wanders off. And she said that just because you got lost doesn't mean you'll never get found.

It'd be nice to believe her.

I just got done being bored off my ass in group therapy. The guy in charge is pathetic. He's also what Meemaw would call ugly as sin.

Now they're saying I'm going to go to another one-on-one meeting. I already know it's a waste of my time, but I've got time to waste, so what the hell? I'll have to see how long it takes the lesbo to give up on me.

I feel like getting in somebody's face, talking some shit. But they've got it set up so that the hour I get my rec in the TV room, everybody else is down in the courtyard for exercise. And when I get to go out there, everybody is inside except the other "special status" offenders like me.

I hate sitting in here, all this thinking. Today Gray Suit said I should start getting materials through the mail from the Houston school district so that I can keep up with my schoolwork. That makes me laugh. I ought to be a junior but I still don't even got the credits to be a sophomore. That's my stupid ass for you.

A girl in another unit killed herself. I don't know how she did it or anything. Everybody is in lockdown for Christ knows how long. Not much of a change for me since I barely see anyone else, anyway. But no group session. What a tragedy.

I can't get how anybody could off herself. Yeah, life is lame as hell, but I still like it. Since what happened with Theo and the other thing, though, sometimes I'm sitting here feeling so guilty and bad that it makes me want to disappear. I guess that when people kill themselves they're really just trying to disappear.

I had this crazy-real dream this morning. It was like from the time before we moved to the Montrose duplex, but even though I'm my right age in it, Theo is just a little puppy like he was when Kevin first bought him. In the dream I come through the door after taking him outside to do his business, and there are these piles of U-Haul boxes scattered everywhere in the living room. Shauna is singing Ella Fitzgerald and taping them together.

I ask her why the boxes are out, but she plays dumb.

I tell her she'd better not tell me that we're moving again, and then I unclip Theo's leash and watch him go crazy sniffing around the boxes, smelling all the houses we've lived in before.

She tells me that she found this great duplex on the other side of town, but I'm not having any of it. I go off on her. "Christ, Shauna! Why do you do this to me? You have no idea what it's like. All you do is think up ways to make my life suck worse!" I start ripping apart boxes. In real life she'd be on me, scratching at me and screaming for me to stop, but in the dream she just picks up the torn boxes and tapes them back together.

She acts all calm, talking fresh starts and new friends. She tells me the place is in the Montrose and acts like I should be all happy to go to Lamar High.

I tell her to screw Lamar, and I mean it. Lamar is all rich white kids. How the hell am I going to fit with them? I tell her I wish I was black or even Mexican instead of white trash like her.

She stops taping boxes together and just stares at me like if she could make me disappear by looking at me, she would.

I tell her I like the friends I have, and I like the North Side. I tell her if she thinks that I'm going to turn into some faggy schoolgirl just because we move, she's whacked off her ass.

She tells me to stop, says she's warning me. And when she says that, I know this is the last time we're going to move for a long time. In the dream, I know something bad is going to happen, but I'm not going to tell her. I'm

not going to tell her shit about the bad feeling I have, be-
cause I want her to see what will happen. And to know
it's all her fault. So I just stare at her hard.

She grabs my wrists with her bony hands and talks
right in my face, asks me, did I ever think for a second
that I might like the change?

That sets me off, and I tell her what I should've told
her lots of other times. That every time we move she
says the same bullshit. But moving won't change any-
thing for us. That I'm still gonna be fucked-up me, and
she's still gonna be fucked-up her.

Red splotches pop up on her too-skinny face, and she
looks like she wants to kill me. She lets go of my arms
and starts throwing empty boxes at me. She says, "Sor-
ry, princess, but you're stuck with me. So shut up and
start packing!"

I woke up from the dream screaming how much I
hate Shauna right into my pillow like I'm seven. The
bitch in the cell next to me was pounding the wall telling
me where to shove my temper tantrum.

It wasn't always like this with Shauna. When I was
little, she had this boyfriend, Kevin. The only one I ever
liked. He even bought this cool house in the suburbs.
We all lived there together. It had a yard with a stone
bunny statue in it. Theo loved that bunny, humped it
all the time. He loved digging holes in the perfect lawn,
too. But Shauna and Kevin split up over some stupid
shit, and there went my normal life.

I just counted it up, and we've moved 19 times in the last 10 years. 19 times. How messed up is that? All the apartments have the same shitty tan carpet, the same white walls we can't paint. The same tiny kitchen with an empty fridge because Shauna's so paranoid about getting fat she won't keep food in the house.

We move so much that we don't even bother to break down the boxes anymore. They just get piled up in the garage or in a closet. Shauna used to sneak Theo in so we wouldn't have to pay the pet deposit. Then we'd throw our shit in the closets, and that was it. It was supposed to be home even though Shauna never put anything up on the walls, never tried to make it feel personal. Even my homeboys who are way poorer than us have moms that put up a crucifix or two, the Virgin of Guadalupe, posters, whatever they have. Something to show that people live in the place, at least.

No matter where we move, there are always liquor stores and alleys that smell like old sex. Shauna gets a different job, but it's always a crap one. She still comes home complaining about filing papers all day, how she got so bored she fell asleep, how the boss chewed her out for it. Or it'll be that waiting tables sucks, guys grab her ass, the cook gives her shit when she turns in special orders, the manager cheats her on tips. She'll still stay out late on her payday and bring home some sleazy guy with a comb-over.

It's amazing just how dumb she is. If moving could fix everything, everybody would do it. But she refuses to see that stupid "fresh start" idea for what it is—complete bullshit.

Once we move, I lose everything I had in the old place. It's a bitch.

I try to stay in with my old friends. I mean, I have a cell phone. Even when I'm grounded, I just take Theo out for a walk and call somebody to pick me up. But things aren't the same when you live far away from your homies—you're not there to know when things go down, you don't know the talk on the street, you slip out of their minds. That's why when Shauna dumps me in a new school I have to find a place to fit in fast. Because I can only take being on my own for so long.

When the cell doors slide open for rec, I barely believe it. I think maybe this is the most I've read in my whole life. I shove the notebook under the mattress and shuffle out to line up with everybody else. I fall in line behind the tall, fat guy who took Baby Tiger's cell. It's times like this that I really miss Tigs, but no way am I going to risk talking to anybody. Maybe that's what got Tigs in trouble. I'm real good at getting people into trouble.

CHAPTER 28: THEN

"Listen, Eddie, thirteen seconds don't sound like long, but when your ass is getting pounded by twenty strong-as-fuck dudes and you can't fight back, it's gonna feel like fuckin' forever, okay?"

Eddie jogged a little in place. "You underestimate me, *carnalito*." He cracked his knuckles and then nodded at the door. "Let's do this."

I kicked open the door to the vacant apartment, grabbed Eddie by the arm, and pushed him inside. Before I even slammed the door behind us, the count started and the homies were yelling and beating on him. Mono locked eyes with me just as his fist smashed into Eddie's gut. I knew what he was waiting for.

"Can you take it, bro? Can you fuckin' take it?" I screamed as I pounded him from behind. "Think you're *Mara* material, *ése*?"

By Poco's call of *cinco*, Eddie was crumpled on the floor taking kicks to his sides and back. I couldn't see his face. Because even though this was the right thing, a hardship he had to go through, I didn't want Eddie to see me hit him. Me getting clicked in, whatever, that was pain to the body. Watching Eddie get jumped hurt me in a different way, a soul-pounding.

Some of the guys from the back pushed forward when Mono called out *ocho*, and I let Doble shove me out of reach of Eddie. As soon as Doble made his first contact with Eddie, I knew giving up my spot was a mistake. Now Doble was pounding him twice as hard. Nobody was supposed to hit your face, but when Poco called out *once*, Doble punched Eddie above the ear. On *doce* he kicked his chin, and on the final count of *trece* he yanked Eddie's head back by the hair and smashed his face forward into the dirty carpet.

"That's it!" Mono shouted a split second too late to save Eddie a broken nose.

Doble yanked Eddie up off the ground and slapped his back. "*Bienvenido*, homie," he said, shoving him too hard.

Eddie wobbled, blood streaming out of his nose. One of his eyes was swollen all the way shut.

"Way to take it, brother," I told him.

"*La Eme Ese controla*," Eddie said. His voice was strong, but something looked loose in his expression. And I had a moment of, oh shit, what'd I do? But then we busted out the Dos Equis and Coronas, plus a rag to clean up his face a little, and the party started.

CHAPTER 29: NOW

Lunch comes early. Gabe slides a tray of neon-orange macaroni and cheese over to me. He's already walking away when he says, "No observation today," so I don't have a chance to ask him how come. Maybe he remembers me telling him what a dummy I am, how long it takes me to read shit. I shovel in the mac and cheese, rinse it down with some weak grape juice, and get back down to business. I'm tired of sitting with the covers over my head, so I slide down under my cot and let the blanket fall down over the edge.

Today group was stupid as hell, but funny. The word we were supposed to talk about was "peace" and it took some of the bitches half the session to figure out he wasn't talking about a gun. Group Guy is a moron, and his teeth make me laugh.

So I was sitting by the fence during my outdoor rec, trying to stay away from the freaks. Except for a couple of Mexican girls by the stairs, it looks like special ed recess. A midget, a kid in a wheelchair, a girl missing an arm, another chick with an eye patch. Not what I want to see during my one hour out of the unit.

I turned my back to the weirdos and looked out past the fence. There's this abandoned stretch of land, and I watched the wind make faded plastic bags dance through the weeds. Then I saw something moving on its own. It was a teeny white and orange cat. It chased a grasshopper for a minute or two, then started crying all pitiful when it couldn't catch it. Dogs are way better than cats, but I still felt sorry for it. Animals aren't bad the way people are. People do wrong and need punishing, but animals don't know any better. They do what they know how to do. I don't see how anybody could hurt an animal.

The cat walked toward the fence, and then it started to climb the chain links about ten feet away from me. I tried to tell it not to come in, that it was better off free, but really I was hoping it would come over so I could pet it. When it got to the barbed wire at the top, the stupid thing stuck its paw right onto the sharp part and yowled. It jumped back to the ground and ran away.

Janet didn't show up for three days in a row, so I was almost glad to see her today. I still acted pissed, but it was good just to get out of the cell. It even seemed like the hour went by faster. I like it best when she has a game for us to play.

I haven't heard shit from anyone in the crew. It's like my homeboys already forgot about me. I wrote two letters to Cartoon, plus one to Slots. And I know my letters make it out. When I write to Meemaw, she always writes back. I can feel myself getting pissed. I'd do anything for them, and they can't send me a fuckin' postcard? Cartoon would say some shit about how I'm just a girl and I can't claim Crazy Crew, so they got no obligation to me. But loyalty goes deeper than rules, and I'm loyal. They should know that by now.

For like the first time since third grade, I'm actually doing my schoolwork. I was a good student when I was little as long as my teachers were cool. I remember my second grade teacher, Ms. Riggins. She was this real tall black lady, and she was always nice to me. Sometimes I'd ask her why couldn't she be my mom? When I came to school she'd say, "Lexi Lou, how are you?" Then she'd laugh, and her pretty white teeth showed.

Third grade was whatever, then in fourth grade shit hit the fan. Mrs. Montes hated me. I was already getting my period and I had boobs and everything. She'd just stare at me like it was my fault I looked like I did. Like I wanted to have boys popping my bra strap and trying to pinch my nipples or girls laughing when I came out of the class bathroom with a dirty pad all wrapped up in toilet paper because there wasn't a trash can in there. I started messing up my work just because it pissed Mrs. Montes off; then before I knew it, they were holding me back. And everything in school sucked after that.

But when the big fat envelope from Lamar High School came last week, I didn't throw it away like I planned. They won't let me have my music or anything in here. I can only stand scribbling in this notebook for so many hours a day. I might as well do something. I bet this is how they get even the stubbornest shits to finish their GED in alternative schools. Just bore the hell out of them until they do something.

All the assignments come with real clear directions, and I'm supposed to get a new package every week. There's even a letter saying that I can request a tutor if I'm having any trouble. Kiss-asses.

Those preppy jerks in the Lamar office didn't give a shit about me when I went in to register in April. But Gray Suit says a lot of people on the outside are blaming Lamar for not doing more to stop what happened. They're just trying to cover themselves, I guess. Whenever the security guards at Lamar heard that something was going down, they just made sure to chase everybody off campus so that we didn't fight on school property.

The school I was in before was the opposite. There were stairwells and certain halls where people got jumped all the time. Nobody cared. There was even a corner of the courtyard that the security cameras didn't reach.

When I transferred to Lamar, I just drifted at first. Then I started to hang at the convenience store where the non-preps and apartment kids smoked after school. That's where I met Cartoon. I saw him from where I was standing by this broke-ass pay phone. I was passing the time drawing designs on my arm in Sharpie, spirals and lines and squiggles to spell out LIFE IS SHIT in my own secret language. I saw him go into the store. Cartoon is skinny but his arms are all built, and that day he had on a wife beater and baggy brown pants slung way low on his hips like he wanted you to think about what would happen if you loosened that red belt even a little.

When he walked back out with his pack of smokes, he came over my way, looking me up and down with this sly smile. He said, "Damn, girl, you look hot in those shorts."

I just gave him my best go-to-hell look and told him to shut up. But when I felt his eyes slide over my tank top I pushed my elbows against the wall a little to make my boobs stick out more. Then I said, "Watch out 'fore I beat your ass."

"You new?" he asked. He smacked his pack of reds against his palm.

"I ain't new, bitch. I'm Lexi," I said, giving him this half smile. And when he offered me one of his smokes, I asked him, "Don't you got anything better?"

He lit up and leaned forward. After a sec, he asked, "What you got in mind?"

By the end of the day, I had my hook-up for handle-bars, plus somebody to hang with. Cartoon introduced me around to his homeboys. And my boys are down. They always make sure I'm okay.

This Cartoon fool, I know him. I mean, I know his type. Strutting around like he's the shit, wearing the colors of his lame-ass gang like he's going to star in some Disney special. Fool doesn't know anything about battling for real. Guys like him, they've got no style, neither. Sure, what dude ain't looking to a score a piece of ass, but have a little style is all I'm saying.

No matter how much you lay it on, though, I guess when it comes to girls it always boils down to: how fast can I get your clothes off? Now that I've got the time to think it over, I feel kind of bad about that. Looking at a female's tits and liking her from there when I don't even know a name. Even with Becca. I got to admit I was thinking "pussy" before I fell in love with her sad smile and that long straight hair begging me to wrap my fingers up in it.

But this Lexi chick is easier than a game of tic-tac-toe. Sticking her tits in everybody's face. Just asking that fool to give her trouble. And wanting the trouble, too, for all I can tell. Like she's saying, "Hey you, got nothing but screwing on your mind? Sweet, so long as you toss some Xanax my way." She's no Becca, that's for sure.

As soon as I think of Becca, it's like somebody punches me in the gut. Making fun of Lexi and her fool boyfriend can't protect me from the fact that I'm the one with my ass in the wringer; I'm the one who doesn't even know what he did or what they're trying to pin on me. Because there's Becca's letter. There's Becca saying good-bye to me like there's no going back.

I've got to keep from falling into that nothing place where I can't think nothing but Becca, Becca, get Becca back. Before I know what I'm doing, I'm pulling the pencil through the springs of the cot above me. I flip to the back of Lexi's notebook and let loose. I guess my brain is all soaked with Lexi's business, because what comes out on the page is her standing outside that convenience store. Just like she said, she's got the Sharpie in her hand, only it's not just her arm that she's marked up. Her whole body is covered with designs and writing, and for a second I think of the *mareros* from El Salvador and Honduras that I met a couple of times, their faces and necks and arms and hands tattooed completely. I keep drawing, and the tattoos climb over her face. Then the designs spill out onto the brick wall behind her, and I realize that she's standing in a pool of ink that comes up to her ankles. I keep drawing, and the ink climbs in spirals halfway up her legs. Her face doesn't change. She's still standing there, her whole body saying, "I'm cool, I'm really fuckin' cool."

"She doesn't know," I say out loud. "She doesn't know that she's in deep."

It freaks me out that I'm talking to myself. I feel kind of shaky, and I put down the pencil real careful this time, making sure not to break it. I'm not sure what the drawing means, but I know I don't like it.

I find my place again in Lexi's notebook and yank it back up in front of my face. I have to push my eyes across the lines. It's slow going, and every word I read has to kick that drawing out of the way before it can hit my brain. But I've got to keep reading.

Here is what I didn't tell Janet about that time Richard took me to McDonald's when I was eight. I didn't tell her that I wore my favorite dress, or that I was disappointed when Richard got there. That he was just an old guy with hairs sticking out of his nose, brown splotches all over his hands, and a greasy bald spot in the middle of his gray head. That Richard let me sit in the front seat and did my seatbelt for me even though I was plenty big enough to do it for myself. That he didn't seem to listen when I answered his questions about my favorite TV shows. That my legs stuck to the leather seat of his big Buick and made a sucking sound when I got out at McDonald's. That I ate my sundae as fast as I could and asked to go home. That he said no and told me to play on the playground. That I didn't want to, but I did it anyway because I thought that then we could leave. That he watched me climb the netting all the way to the top of the play set. That when I came down the slide, he was waiting for me at the bottom and smiling. That I didn't like his smile. That he picked me up and carried me over to an empty bench and sat me in his lap even though I was too big for that. That he just laughed when I tried to get down. That I felt something inside Richard's pants press against me, something that made me feel dirty even though at the time I didn't . know what it was.

I didn't tell Janet because I've never told anybody.

I wrote Cartoon another letter, and toward the end I reminded him of what a good time we had, just him and me. I write dirty stuff for him because I know he likes it. Meemaw is always telling me I need friends who are girls, but chicks hate me. It's basically automatic. Girls hate anybody that boys like. And boys like me.

I use what I've got, I'm not gonna lie. I make sure my shorts pull tight across my butt, and I wear my tank tops so that plenty of tit shows. Shauna is always trying to say I ought to lose weight, what a knockout I'd be if I did, but no way am I gonna give up Meemaw's goodies just to have a flat belly. I get plenty of looks the way I am now.

It's the being wanted that I like, hands and eyes drawn to my body like magnets. Yeah, when I'm walking along and boys are talking about my ass, I act all pissed. But I love it. It makes me feel powerful, like I could karate-chop my way through the whole world right then.

I love being sexy, but I don't love sex. Maybe it's because of Richard. Maybe it's because Shauna took me to get on the Pill when I was thirteen. She said it was for my cramps, but I know it was because she thought I was already doing it. Sex has never been that exciting to me. When I'm actually with a guy and he's doing his thing, it's like waiting for laundry to finish or trying to get through the last five minutes of Meemaw's church without falling asleep. Anyway, lots of people don't really like sex. What matters is knowing how to pretend that you do.

I make lots of noise and grab the dude's hips. Make him think he's driving me crazy. Pull him close, shout some shit, give him a little nip on the ear. Guys are so sure that they're the shit, they never think you might be faking.

The first guy I kissed was this real sweet kid I knew when I was ten and we lived out in La Porte. Nestor. He had this cute gap between his teeth and long eyelashes. He was always a gentleman, holding my hand and stuff, kissing me with closed lips, never trying to touch me anywhere. He was all the time telling me how smart I was and helping me out at school. That was when Meemaw lived with us, and she always said that Nestor was good people.

Me and Nestor lost touch after a couple of moves, and it wasn't until last year that I found out he got leukemia when he was thirteen. And he died from it. Dead.

I felt so pissed that I hadn't been there for him, that I hadn't sat by his bed and told him jokes to make him forget about losing his hair and the tubes in his arms. I wonder if he died a virgin.

I already finished all the sweets Meemaw sent in her package. I've been in here long enough to know how to cry so nobody can hear me, and I'm getting by without pills. But I haven't figured out how to make Meemaw's cookies and donuts last me the week. It doesn't matter how much she sends, two days and it's gone. Because when you're stuck in a little room with nothing to do, how are you going to keep yourself from pulling that box out from under the bed and scarfing down another peanut butter cookie?

All that's left in the box now is her note. She didn't write much, just "I love you and am praying for you." She sends me these cards with Bible verses and little sayings on them. They've got a sticky side like a bumper sticker so you can put them on the wall or something. Here's one.

"Come now and let us reason together," says the Lord. "Though your sins are like scarlet, they shall be as white as snow."—Isaiah 1:18

Free! Free! As soon as we give over our hearts to the Lord, we are free! Free from shame, guilt, fear, and all the darkness that once surrounded us! Praise the Lord!

I want to tell Meemaw that I have that whole Bible she sent me, so she shouldn't waste her stickers on me. But that would hurt her feelings.

Those words belong to some other world. I mean, I can read them. I'm not stupid. But it's like reading a poster on the bus. This stuff is real to Meemaw, but it's not real to me. All those exclamation points just make me want to laugh. Meemaw might as well send me quotes from the Driver's Ed manual. Or the phone book.

I guess after these weeks of group I'm kind of used to it, and maybe I even like it a little. But I still don't say anything. Today when all the girls were telling what was what about their past, how they felt alone or apart and shit, I wanted to say something. I almost did, too, but it was like there was this invisible hand clamped over my mouth. I couldn't do it. Just couldn't.

I wanted to say, you know how sometimes the thing that sticks with you isn't that big a deal, or it wouldn't seem like it to anybody else, but to you it stands for everything that's busted up and sucky in your life? If I had any balls, I would've told about this one time when I was maybe eight and Meemaw made me go into the big church with her on Sunday.

Before that I stayed in the children's room. I was bigger than the other kids, but I was kind of like a helper to the teacher lady. And I never wanted to leave. Always music playing and juice and graham crackers. I remember all the toys had the name of the church written on them in Sharpie. The Pentecostal Way Living Water Church. Like who was going to steal toys from a church?

Anyway, Meemaw dragged me into the main church room that day. There was singing, which I liked because I have a good voice just like my mom. Then they prayed and this guy in a cheesy white suit talked for a long time. The whole time people were shouting Amen from all sides.

I had my head on Meemaw's shoulder and I was thinking up new moves for the number-one song on Mega 101 when the preacher called for people to come down to the front, to come down to the altar and be healed of darkness and washed of sin. I looked around and all of a sudden lots of people were crying and shaking. One lady's false eyelashes were halfway down her cheek. A man fell into the aisle and started saying things I couldn't understand. A woman in front of us swished her green skirt back and forth. Then she started dancing with her hands lifted.

And the thing is, even though it was crazy, with everybody in their own world like you'd see at a rave, they all looked so happy. Peaceful and excited at the same time, like they could hear some special music that I couldn't. I looked over at Meemaw, and she was crying *the same happy tears. I kept waiting for her to look at me, but she didn't. Like she didn't even remember I was there.*

I felt like I was the only one in the whole place who was empty inside. When I was a little kid, I prayed with Meemaw for Jesus to come into my heart, and I'd done it a bunch of times at different summer camps and revivals. Because I never felt sure that it'd really stuck. That was the day that I knew it hadn't. I was standing there all alone with no Jesus in my heart.

I don't want to feel sorry for her, not even when I read about her sicko dad messing with her. I know if somebody tried to mess with Regina, I'd blow his ass right off the map, but I still want to tell Lexi to forget the boo-hoo, poor-little-white-girl bullshit. She's never been hungry. She's never gotten a beating. She's never been on the run from *la migra* or the CPS. She's never had to pack a baby sister off to California just to keep her safe. I want to write, TELL ME WHAT THE FUCK YOU KNOW ABOUT ME in Sharpie across every single page of her little diary.

But reading Lexi's notebook also makes me think how everybody is off the record in a way. Not just fools like my pops who didn't get their papers straightened out. Not just dropouts like me and Eddie wanting to stay out of the system. I mean that whole part inside of you that nobody else even knows is there. There's a Lexi that talks trash to Janet, a Lexi that crosses her arms in group, a Lexi that writes in her journal. But there's also this Lexi that nobody knows about, a Lexi inside of Lexi. That's how somebody can be getting high or going to church but at the same time still feel like a seven-year-old kid locked out of the swimming pool. That's how I can be clicking Eddie in, kicking the shit out of him but somewhere deep inside feel that I'm still his *hermanito*. Down there, there's a little guy who just wants us to go home and make some ketchup sandwiches.

CHAPTER 30: NOW

I wake up to the sound of Gabe knocking the bars of my cell with a meal tray. For a second, I'm tripping because I think it's breakfast and he's going to take the notebook away. When I scramble out from under my cot tent, though, I see the steak fingers and corn, and I know it must be dinner. I take the tray and thank Gabe, but he just raises his eyebrows and shakes his head like he's saying, the clock is ticking and why am I taking naps on the job?

I watch him walk away and think how his white hair is dry and fluffy just like this troll doll me and Eddie bought for Regina one time when my Tía Julia came to visit and took us all to Wal-Mart. It was a hippie troll with a little green suit, and she put those clothes on and took them off about a million times a day. When she was tired or upset, she'd suck on its hair until it was all one big slobbery spike. We made fun of her for it, but after she went to Cali, I would have given anything to see her curled up watching TV and sucking on her troll doll.

Now I swallow the corn in three bites and take the steak fingers with me under the cot. I'm about to duck under the blanket when I see the guy in Tiger's old cell give me a look.

"*Y qué, cabrón?*" I say. "It won't be long till you get what it's like." But I can't tell if he even hears me. And I don't have time to care.

A while back Janet and me played Scrabble, and then when I got sick of it, I just messed around with the tiles. I ended up making his name. It felt like it was on accident, but it also felt right. Like just exactly what I ought to spell out.

At first I just sat there staring at his name, thinking about how I first found out what it was. Gray Suit tossing photos and information sheets over to me in the conference room. His name on the page there like it was nothing.

Janet asked if I knew what Azael meant, and when I said no, she said she'd find out for me. Since then I've pissed her off more than once, and I thought probably she wouldn't tell me even if she did find out. Then today she gave me a little piece of paper with some information on it. The main meaning she found for the name was "Angel of Death" or "Avenging Angel." She said some magician wrote a long time ago about how the fallen angel Azael was tied up in the desert and tortured for everything he did.

I wonder what Janet thought when she read that.

What sucks today:
#1 – My hair is greasy as hell.
#2 – Powdered eggs for breakfast again.
#3 – No mail.
#4 – I haven't been outside for three days. Fuckin rain.
#5 – My toilet backed up.
#6 – The cell smells like shit. Big time.
#7 – I'm thinking about him.

Today I started to tell Janet. Started to tell her just like I practiced it with Gray Suit. She brought some Play-Doh again, and I was mashing it in my hands. Halfway through my little performance, though, Janet took the Play-Doh out of my hand and put it away.

She gave me a dirty look and said, "That's not you talking. Save that bull for your lawyer." Then she just left me sitting there even though there were fifteen minutes before our time was up.

I should be doing my algebra problems so I can mail them in tomorrow, but my mind just drifts. Mostly I think about things that have to do with him.

Once I saw his name canned on a train car. There's this spot on Montrose by some tracks where Cartoon and Slots liked to smoke and check out what was new in the pieces rolling by. On the trains you could see what gangs all the way out in LA were doing and who they were fighting, just by how they tagged up the rail cars. Plus there were lots of writers doing throw-ups that had nothing to do with gangs. People just wanting to make their mark. Slots likes to pretend he's an original, but I could tell he got lots of his ideas just by studying their shit.

Slots started going on about this one piece way before I could see it. My eyes aren't great. I'm supposed to wear glasses, but I never have. I can see good enough without them.

So anyway, when the train got closer, I could see what he was talking about. It was this design of a cloud that had bullets coming out of it. The curves of the cloud spelled out "R.I.P. Pájaro" in light blue letters. If you looked real hard, you could see that the puddles the bullets were falling into spelled out "Azael."

Me and Slots were still talking about the piece when Cartoon started walking alongside the train, shaking up a can of brown paint.

I told him not to mess with it, that I liked that one. Slots was on my side, too, but Cartoon said, "This loser's canning for MS-13. You can tell by the blue and shit. Why should I respect that?"

There was nothing I could say to change his mind, and then it was too late because Cartoon was already spraying over the piece with a sloppy Crazy Crew tag.

So I just sat back down and took a hit off their joint. When Cartoon came back over to us, I asked him for some bars. Then I just drifted, listening to them talk shit and staring through the ugly brown tag to that light blue cloud raining bullets. I watched all the different colors swirl together. By the time the train rounded the bend and passed out of sight, I was floating on my own cloud of nothing.

I remember canning that boxcar like it was yesterday. It was a while after Pájaro got cut down, but a busted-up feeling was still dogging me all the time. I did the design in my black book, then found a good spot on a boxcar in one of the train yards by Beto's house. I went by myself that time, nobody to slap me on the back and tell me it was awesome. So I always wondered, did anybody see it? I'd like to beat down this Cartoon fool for disrespecting my artwork and dissing Pájaro's memory. At the same time, though, I'm just glad somebody saw it first, even if it had to be wasted on Lexi and her little punk friends.

Gray Suit's been coming twice a week lately because the trial starts in a month. All he does is drill me on my testimony. He even asked me if I could make myself cry.

I told him to piss off. By now he's used to me, so he didn't react. He just told me that if I don't get this right, I'm the one who'll be screwed.

I've been thinking about that for a long time. But I also keep going back to what Janet said. I think about how bad it feels to fake things, like all the times I've pretended to cum just to make a dude feel good. Just the idea of forcing tears down my cheeks in front of a bunch of strangers in a courtroom pisses me off.

There's faking, and then there's faking.

There's no reason for me to be thinking about him. No fuckin reason. He's nothing to me. So what if I know what his name means? So what if I saw a train with his name canned on it? Everybody does what they have to do, that's just how it is.

But today, when Group Guy asked us to talk about who we feel closest to, I thought, him. How twisted is that, for me to think of Azael out of everybody in the whole world? When I didn't even know his name before?

Even once I thought about how messed up it was, I still couldn't get myself to think of anybody else. I know I have Meemaw. And Shauna, sort of. Maybe Janet, just a little. I used to have Cartoon and Slots. But none of them feel close. When I'm alone in here, they seem way far off, tiny specks like fleas.

Azael's big in my mind. Sometimes I'm lying here, and I think about that cloud crying bullets that maybe he painted, and I start thinking that things could have been different. If I'd lived in a different place. If I'd met him before Cartoon. If we got high together, even. I've known a lot of jerks I thought were my friends, but maybe he'd have been a real one. Maybe.

All these ifs and maybes set off a lot of crazy stuff in my head, and even thinking of poor Theo doesn't make me stop wondering about Azael.

I want to tell her that she's fucking crazy, that she doesn't know me, that I don't care about her. But I can't, because no matter how hard I try to think of Regina or Eddie or Becca, I know that Lexi's the one who's most real to me now. When I close my eyes, she's what I see. Not just a girl with big tits and blow-job lips, but somebody whose life is tangled up in mine somehow.

I think about what Pakmin said, how she doesn't know I'm watching her. Maybe he's telling the truth, but it feels like she's the only one who still sees me.

Janet's after me all the time to talk about it. When she starts up, I try to go someplace else in my mind. I think of Meemaw and how good it would feel to put my head in her lap so she could play with my hair and talk to me like when I was little, like she used to do when I got real sad. She'd play with my hair and I'd put my ear against her tummy and listen to it rumble, press my face against her T-shirt and smell the Tide and Downy. She would sing to me, too. A church song or maybe something by Johnny Cash.

I miss her touch so much. I'd do anything to feel her hug me tight.

Only two weeks before the trial starts. When Gray Suit came to see me today, I kept to myself, did what he told me to, and didn't give him attitude. He gave me a funny look and asked if I was okay. He told me not to worry, said that we're ready. Absolutely ready, he said. Slimy smile on his face.

I nodded and even smiled back, playing the good-girl witness like I'm supposed to. But it made me feel sick. Liar. Liar. Deserves to be on fire. *That's what I hear in my head every time I go over the testimony with him. You can practice a lie until it rolls off your tongue like the truth, but it still leaves you feeling dirty.*

Six months ago you couldn't have paid me enough money to do my homework, and now I'm so stressed out that I've done every single assignment for the whole week, and it's only Wednesday. That's some kind of messed up.

One week left. I don't know what to do with myself, so I get down on my knees and crawl under the sink. I run my fingers over what I carved there back when I thought I'd only be here for a few days, a week at the most. Back when I was still Sexi Lexi.

It doesn't seem real now. All those letters to Cartoon and Slots, and not a single reply.

I picture myself up on the stand in the skirt and jacket Meemaw bought for me, probably off the sale rack in the old ladies' section of Dillard's. I picture the judge telling me to put my hand on a Bible.

I'm scared shitless. Scared I'll say what Gray Suit told me to, scared I won't.

My head hurts from staring at her writing for so long, but when I get to the last page she's written on, I get this tight feeling in my chest. What trial is she talking about? Is she the one getting charged, or is she just testifying? There's more questions than answers here, and time is running out on me fast.

Whatever Lexi's up to, it's no good for me. But I know her fuck-ups and her moods, her silences and her scribblings. Already, I know her too much to hate her. She's just a scared shit like Eddie or me or anybody, trying not to show how messed up she is.

It's no excuse for her bullshit. On the outside we'd be enemies. But in here, I need her. I need her to keep writing, to figure her shit out. I need her to be okay, to do right. Because if she doesn't, I'm the one who'll pay. That much I know.

Praying ain't the answer. I kick the problem over in my mind for a minute. I think about writing her a note, but as soon as my fingers close around the pencil, I start drawing in her notebook again. This time it's a knife. Not one I recognize, though. It looks like something out of a

Star Trek fan's nightmare. A make-believe knife, a fucking toy. It's not really made for fighting. It has a black handle in the middle and jagged blades that curve up out of the handle on both sides like horns. I've seen knives like this in junky neighborhood stores that sell shit to anybody who's got ten bucks. A little case of knives alongside the glow-in-the-dark condoms, energy pills, and steel wool for crack pipes.

Each line from the pencil finds its place easy; I don't even have to erase. I wonder about Lexi getting her notebook back and finding the drawing. Will she think it's a threat? Or is she the only one who'll know what it means?

I finish the triangular cutouts on the blades just as the light in the cell clicks off. I'm putting the pencil back under the mattress when my fingers brush against something metal. Becca's necklace. Last week I unwrapped it from the wad of tape on her letter. I fold my hand around it and pull it out. The butterfly is cold against my skin, and I wrap the chain around my fingers. Using the light from the hall, I lay Becca's necklace on the same page where I drew the knife. I fold the paper in from the edges and wrap it up tight around the necklace until there's a little package tucked against the notebook's spiral. The knife and the butterfly. I'm counting on Lexi to know what they mean.

It takes me a long time to fall asleep. While I'm waiting, I apologize to Becca in my head, promising her a new necklace if she'll just take me back when I get out of here.

CHAPTER 31: NOW

When Gabe brings breakfast, I hand him last night's empty dinner tray with the notebook underneath it. He takes it without saying anything about the little bulge from the necklace.

I lie on the cot and stare at the ceiling until it's time for rec. Out in the courtyard, I'm too out of it to do push-ups, so I just stare into the abandoned land past the fence. I wonder if maybe I'll see Lexi's kitten. But I don't. Probably it got eaten by something. As a kind of experiment, I try feeling sorry for the cat.

It doesn't work. I end up thinking about lunch.

Back in my cell. I think for sure I'm going to find out something from Lexi when Pakmin comes to get me for observation, but he never does.

I make sure I'm awake when Gabe comes with the dinner tray.

"Hey, Gabe, how come I ain't had observation? Pakmin quit on me or what?"

Gabe scratches his cottony white hair and shifts some cartons of apple juice around in his cart. "Hard to say, son," he says finally, "but it's chicken-fried steak tonight." He hands me the tray with a piece of breaded grayish meat and some green beans before he shuffles on down the hall.

Looking at the drawings in my black book is what I do to calm myself down and make the time pass. It's like my rosary. But it's a rosary missing the last bead. One blank page left in the notebook, and I can't decide what to put there. When I think about what comes out every time I try to draw, I get a sick feeling in my gut.

I leave my pencil under the mattress.

CHAPTER 32: THEN

I was putting buckets and gloves into my cart like I was just a regular shopper when Eddie finally came strolling in. He had a list of cans he was supposed to help me rack for this piece I was going to do for Becca. I had it all planned out, explained to him what to do a million times. But instead of going straight to the paint aisle like I told him, fat-ass Eddie wandered over to the snack section. He started shoving Slim Jims into his pocket, not even noticing that the hardware store clerk was staring right at him.

I locked eyes with the black guy behind the counter and shook my head like I couldn't believe what I was seeing. "Hey, *cabrón*, you got to pay for those," I said plenty loud for the clerk to hear. I walked over to Eddie like I was trying to show him that I was serious. Once I got closer, I dropped my voice and told him in Spanish to pay for something and buy me some time. Then I said louder, "For real, man. Put 'em back or pay for 'em." By then, the black guy was out from behind the counter and coming over to the aisle.

Eddie made a big deal of pulling shit out of his pocket. He tossed all but one package of beef jerky back on the shelf. Then he grabbed a bag of chips.

"You ready to pay?" the clerk asked.

"Yeah, yeah," Eddie said.

They walked over to the counter together, the black dude watching him like a hawk the whole way.

While the clerk was busy with Eddie, I walked real casual over to the spray paint aisle. I packed the cans into the waistband of my pants. It was January, so I had on Pelón's big-ass Colts jacket. That made it easy to hide the cans, but I still couldn't get everything I needed without Eddie's help. *Pinche* Eddie and his snacks.

After Eddie left the store, I zipped up my jacket and walked up to the front with my cart. I parked it near the counter.

"Boss forgot to give me the money for his supplies," I said. I knew the clerk would believe me because sometimes the guy I painted apartments for really did send me here to buy rollers and drop cloths.

Then I was out the door and ready to kick Eddie's stupid ass.

"What the fuck, man." I gave Eddie a shove when I caught up with him. "You were supposed to be helping me rack some *pinche* cans."

"Easy, little bro. Come on, I made you a diversion and shit, like in the movies, right?" Eddie laughed and offered me his half-eaten beef jerky.

I pushed his hand away. "Why the shit do you think I gave you my backpack and the list of colors? I still ain't got the cans I need. Now I got to hit up another store. And you were about to get your ass caught for shoplifting. You can't be wasting your time on beef jerky, *pendejo*."

"Look, I bought you some Cheetos." Eddie pulled out the package.

"*A la verga*, dumbass," I said, but I took the chips. "You're coming with me to Home Depot, and you better not get lost in the snacks. I got to do the piece tonight so I can surprise my girl with it."

"*Cálmate*, Azz," Eddie said. "I promise I'll do it right this time."

CHAPTER 33: NOW

I hang my head over the john and puke my guts out. It's the third time this morning, and it's not even breakfast yet. When I'm finally done, I rinse my mouth out and then wipe it with the back of my hand. I'm so dizzy I barely make it to the cot. There's an ache deep inside my muscles. I try to sleep, but I can't. It's like an iron hand is squeezing my guts. I lie there with my eyes closed and feel the sweat bead up on my neck and face.

The sound of the breakfast cart and Gabe's shuffling step is sweet music to me. I must look pretty bad because Gabe asks me what's wrong before I even tell him I'm sick.

"Just woke up with my insides in a mess. Feels like I've got a hangover from too many hits of this place." I try to smile.

Gabe shakes his head and puts two extra pieces of toast on my tray. "Drink plenty of water, now," he says. "You've got to hurry up."

He's pointing a shaky finger at last night's dinner tray, so at first I think he means I shouldn't take so long handing it to him.

"Here," I say.

"You don't get it, son. You got to make some choices." He gives me this look like I ought to know what he means.

"Gabe—"

"Time's running real short," he says.

I feel what he means even though I can't understand it with my head. I want to hurry, but I don't know how. I lie back down on the cot and fall asleep chewing the crust of the toast. Dreams swarm over me like flies. Most of them are dark, and the me that's dreaming is praying I will forget them before I wake up.

• • •

I'm sick for two whole days, slipping in and out of a crazy, tripping sleep. At first I'm too out of it to care, but once I feel a little better, I realize that Pakmin hasn't come to see me even once. On the third day, I ask Gabe about it when he brings breakfast. He frowns and repeats the stuff about hurrying up. But before he leaves I make him promise to see what he can do.

Another day passes without a visit from Pakmin, and I start to get scared that my days of observing are over. How am I supposed to figure anything out from my cell? What do they expect me to do?

Finally Pakmin shows up. I'm curled up under the blanket half asleep with my black book tucked between my legs when I hear his footsteps. I barely have time to hide my stuff before he gets to my cell.

Even though it feels like it's been ages since I saw him, he acts like nothing's different. Like I haven't been going crazy in here. I watch his face for any changes, but he keeps it blank. He lets me into the observation room and then leaves without saying a word.

Lexi's in the meeting room across the table from Janet. I'm kind of pissed to be walking in on the middle of the session, but I'm not about to complain. I pull one of the plastic chairs close to the window and listen.

"What about family?" Janet is saying.

"Mostly I think about him," Lexi says.

"Your father?" Janet asks.

"No, *him*. Azael. I think about him a lot."

"As family?"

Lexi shrugs. "I don't know what as. He's just there. I can't stop thinking about him. What do you think that means?"

"It means you're telling the truth about your feelings, for one thing," Janet says.

"You think that really matters? Saying how you feel?"

"It's the starting place for knowing—for knowing who you are. And that's everything." She stretches her thick arms out, and I can see the big sweat rings under her armpits. I can tell that Lexi notices, too, because she looks away. But she doesn't say anything about it.

"You know what I feel the worst about?" Lexi says.

"What?"

"After everything that happened, I went and ate Mexican food with my friends. Had chips and salsa and talked shit like nothing was different, like nobody—I don't know why I did that."

Janet watches her for a minute. "Would you do it again?"

There's a moment of silence, then Lexi shakes her head. Just barely, but she does. "The people I did it for, I haven't heard from them. Nothing. Like I don't even exist to them. But knowing that, knowing they don't care about me, it doesn't change anything. You still can't take things back."

"No, you can't. But you can own up to your mistakes."

"But who to? Who do you tell?"

"That one's on you, Lexi."

"Maybe I could—"

I'm holding my breath, thinking, this is it, this is finally it. Here's where I find out what's going on. But then some middle-aged guy busts into the room, and a tall guard comes in behind him. The first man is wearing a suit. Is this the guy Lexi calls Gray Suit? His face looks like a tomato, and he's moving so fast that his tie whips behind him.

"What the hell do you think you're doing?" he shouts at Janet. He's got Lexi's notebook in one hand. He turns to her for a second. "Not another word, Lexi. This session is over!"

I stand up and put my hands on the window. I look hard at the notebook that the suit is waving around. I wonder, is the necklace in there? I wonder, what did he see in what she wrote that I missed? Then I remember that I've been out for a couple of days. She's had the notebook back for a while. Plenty of time to take the necklace out. Plenty of time to write more. But what did she write?

"How could you do this to her?" he demands, getting right in Janet's face. His mouth moves like he's chewing on his own lip.

"Stop it, stop it!" Lexi shouts at the suit, but he doesn't listen to her.

"Do you want her to stay locked up? Is that your idea?" he asks Janet.

Janet's face goes white. "What are you talking about? I only—"

"I know what you did!" The suit slams the journal down on the table. "Get up, Lexi. You won't be seeing her again."

"You can't do that!" Lexi protests. "No way. Janet's helping me. I'm finally getting my shit together. It's for real. I—"

"Get up!" he repeats.

When she doesn't, he grabs her by the wrists and pulls her up. He turns back to Janet. "What you did is so unprofessional, so outside the bounds of your position. I'm going to see to it that you never pull a stunt like this again."

"All I wanted was to show her how to be honest with herself," Janet says real quiet, never taking her eyes off of him.

Then the suit and the guard are dragging Lexi out of there. She's crying hard, and she shouts over her shoulder, "I'm sorry, Janet!"

I don't even get what any of it means. I feel like I'm about to fall over a cliff, but I don't know which way to step to stay safe. What does Lexi know about me? What did she see?

I walk to the other end of the observation room and stare through the window onto Lexi's empty cell. I think, don't do me wrong, Lexi. Please don't. I think about Eddie and how he needs me on the outside. I think about winning Becca back. I think about Regina and how I don't want her to have to tell her friends that her big brother is locked away for good. It's almost like praying except, really, I know I'm just talking to myself. I keep it up even when Lexi comes back and falls crying onto her bed. After a while, she gets out a pen and starts scribbling inside the pages of a fat book with the covers stripped off, probably her grandma's Bible. I guess the suit kept her notebook, but she's still got to write. I draw to know my mind. Lexi writes to know hers.

After maybe an hour, Lexi's mom, the pretty woman with dark hair, comes into the cell with the suit. It's just the three of them, no guard. Who knows how they got permission to have a visit like that, but anything's possible if you're white.

The man goes on for a long time about how Janet is crazy, how she's trying to ruin Lexi's life. He says how Lexi's testimony is key in the trial, how she's got to know every word of it perfectly. He says the same things over and over. Lexi nods, even says "yes, sir" once, but I think his words are rolling right off of her. Or maybe I just hope they are.

Then her mom starts in. "Listen, Lex, Mr. VanVeldt told me what happened. You've got to think hard about this. Do you really understand the charges? Do you understand what can happen if they find you guilty? You've got to think hard, peanut."

Lexi bites her lip and looks her mother in the eye. But this time I don't think she's trying to pick a fight. This time, I think she's just trying to get her mom to see her. Really see her.

"Look, honey," the mom says, softer now, "I believe in telling the truth, but maybe you should tell God the truth and trust your lawyers about court. You're scaring me, sweetie."

Lexi stands up and walks over to her mother, placing her hands on her shoulders. "I love you, Mom," she says. It's the first time she hasn't called her mom "Shauna," at least as long as I've been watching. And from the look on her mom's face, I'm guessing she hasn't said "I love you" in a long time.

"Can I see Meemaw?" Lexi asks. "In here, like this?"

Lexi's mom looks at the man in the suit. He just throws up his hands.

. . .

When Pakmin leads me out of the observation room, I wish I could talk to him, ask him questions, but I'm afraid of giving away how little I know. From watching Lexi and her mom, I know she's being tried for something, but I don't know what it is—or what she has to gain by dragging me into her shit. For now, the question is, will she frame me, or won't she? What I really want to know is what I can do about it. Or is this part of some sicko torture where I've got to watch myself get screwed over?

CHAPTER 34: NOW

It's been two days since Pakmin came for me. Sometimes he passes by on his way to get other guys, but when I call to him, he acts like he can't hear me.

I get lonely, especially when I wake up first thing in the morning. It gets harder and harder for me to remember what it felt like to be out in the world, free to move around, touch people, eat whatever I want. Sometimes I imagine what it would be like just to hear a familiar voice. Not to be free or anything, just to have that sound in my ears. First I think of Becca, her laugh all sweet and low.

But that always makes me sadder, so I decide to imagine someone I wouldn't get to see even if I was on the outside. I think about dialing the number for my Grams out in Cali and asking for Regina. But this place even messes with my daydreams, because when I imagine Abue picking up, things go wrong.

"*Quién habla?*" she asks me.

"It's me, Azael."

"Who?" Abue asks again. "You must have the wrong number." Then she hangs up. When Gabe brings me breakfast, I want to ask him, what does it mean if not even my grandma remembers me? But I don't. I take the tray without saying anything. I sit on the cot and eat my banana and cereal.

. . .

Finally Pakmin comes for me. "Where you been?" I ask him.

He ignores my question. "This one might be your last, my friend," he says when he lets me into the observation room.

I walk straight to the window onto Lexi's cell. No time for kicking back in the crappy plastic chairs now.

Instead of her county issues, she's wearing a skirt and a jacket, high-heeled shoes. She sits on the edge of her bed combing through her wet hair with her fingers. Her hands fall like she's forgotten what she's doing, and her eyes are all red and puffy. She looks around the room until her gaze finally settles on the corner of the room where the sink is. When she kneels down, I realize that she's unscrewing one of the bolts that anchors the toilet to the concrete. Once she's got it loose, she gets down under the sink. That's where she carved her name. I remember that from her notebook. If I squint, I can even make out the double lines of the S and the L together.

The wannabe badass formerly known as Sexi Lexi is looking shaky as shit this morning. She steadies one hand against the concrete blocks, then starts scratching. She's spelling something out when there's a knock and her door opens. She palms the bolt and spins around all surprised, but it's just her grandmother. So she's not really busted.

"Meemaw." She says it like it's the best word in the whole English language. "Meemaw."

Her grandma comes over to her, helps her up, pulls the bolt out of her hand, and then hugs her tight and long. "You ready, sweetie?" she asks when she finally lets go.

Lexi shakes her head no and bites her lip. She crosses to the desk and pulls a crumpled piece of notebook paper from behind a book.

"Will you help me with this?" she asks. She pulls out the necklace. It's the butterfly.

The grandma takes it from Lexi. "Where'd you get it?" She links the chain around Lexi's neck.

"A friend, I think," Lexi says.

Then the grandma gives her a pair of glasses. They're the finishing touch, I realize. Now Lexi looks like some sweet local girl you'd see working in a grocery store. The angry girl I've been watching for weeks is gone. And for sure nobody'd look at her and think "criminal" or "liar."

Lexi and her grandma walk out. Before the light goes off in the cell, I see what Lexi was scratching on the wall under the sink, even though she didn't get to finish:

CHAPTER 35: THEN

"Cut it out! You're wasting my cans." I pried a can of Red Devil Flame Red out of Pelón's hand and yanked away the plastic bag he had pressed over his nose and mouth.

"Fuck you, man," he said, but he didn't put up a fight. "What's it to you if I have a little fun while you're getting your art on?"

"Nothing, except that's all the red I got, and I still need it. And I need you to hold that flashlight for me. You can have all you want when I'm done, *vale*?"

We were behind this abandoned garage a couple of blocks from the Bel-Lindo, and I was working on a piece for Becca because it was almost our two-month anniversary. The whole back side of the building was blank, so I had lots of room to work. The design was already set: a big-ass A and a big-ass B with a rose growing up around them and holding them together, plus a cartoon Becca with her shoulders against the B, leaning back all sexy with a rose in her hand. I spent forever getting it just right, sketching it out on notebook paper before I inked it into my black book. Now all I had to do was get it up.

It took me almost six hours, but we got lucky and nobody came around or chased us off. By the time I was finished, Pelón was stoned off his ass. I didn't take any hits, but I got a nice high just from all the fumes coming off the wall.

"That shit is tight," Pelón said, laughing all crazy and kind of dancing around in front of my piece. "Becca's gonna shit herself she's gonna like it so much."

Me and Pelón went and partied at Mono's house. I waited until about seven and then changed my clothes and walked over to Becca's apartment. I was thinking sunrise surprise, but it didn't work out like I hoped. Even though it was crazy early, she couldn't get away.

"Sorry, Azz," she said. "The folks are gone, and I got to watch the *pinche* kids all day." Inside I could see her little brothers and sisters, maybe a cousin or two, all lined up in their sleeping bags on the living room floor.

"Just ten minutes, baby. Come on, they're all asleep anyway. I'll have you back before they know you were gone." I leaned down and kissed the back of her neck. "I got something to show you that you're gonna like."

"You always got something I like, Azz, but you're gonna have to give it to me here," she said. She hooked her fingers through the loops of my jeans with a wicked smile.

It wasn't until the next day that I finally got to take her to see it. I had two wine coolers in my bag along with my gear. Before we got to the garage, I pulled out a bandanna and tied it over her eyes.

"Just fuckin' show me, Azz," she said, but I could tell she liked the game.

I led her along the side of the garage and through the tall weeds, making a big deal of guiding her around an old junked-out washing machine.

"Get ready," I said as we came around to the back of the garage, but I stopped cold when I saw the wall.

"Fuck!" I shouted.

"Shit! *Qué pasó?*" Becca pulled the bandanna down around her neck so she could see.

I ignored her and ripped into my backpack. The first thing I landed on was one of the wine coolers, and I pitched it at the empty, gray wall. The shattering glass helped loosen the knot in my throat. "Fuckin' hell," I moaned.

"Azz! Talk to me, what the hell happened?"

"They buffed it. It's barely been two days and somebody fuckin' buffed my piece. See?" I pointed from the blank wall to the drips of gray paint on the grass. "They just painted right over it."

Becca stared at the ground, then she nodded slowly. "*Pendejos*," she said. "What've they got against a little color?"

She walked over and grabbed my backpack, pulling out the other wine cooler. "But it's not this guy's fault. We got to save him." She was trying to make me laugh.

"I've still got the drawing," I said, grabbing for my black book. I flipped to the page. "See? It was like this. But the piece was like a thousand times better."

"It's okay, Azz, I love it." Becca got up on her tiptoes and kissed me. But I couldn't let it go; she never even got to see what I did for her. How it looked up on the wall.

I pulled away from her and reached into my bag. After a second, my hand closed around the can I was looking for. Krylon Camouflage Black. The flattest shit you can get, practically impossible to scrub out. Sticks so good, it's like painting a hole into the wall. It would take the fuckers at least three coats to paint over it. I shook the shit out of that can until I wasn't thinking anymore, and all that mattered was that sweet click and roll. And then with big, sloppy letters, I canned "FUK YOU" all over that wall and everything near it.

Becca kept trying to touch me, telling me to quit it, saying it was okay, that she liked the drawing, that it made her happy, that she didn't need to see it up on a wall. Even though I heard her, I didn't stop until all my cans ran out.

CHAPTER 36: NOW

The hours crawl by. I know I should be figuring some shit out, but nothing happens to help me out. No visits from Pakmin. No observations. No notebook from Gabe. No word about Lexi. Nothing. Just breakfast, rec, lunch, then dinner.

So I think about Lexi, about what she might be saying in court. Her ass is in a bind, and everybody wants her to pin something on me. I imagine her biting her lip, eyes wide and innocent behind those glasses she never wore before. I see a jury already turning soft toward her.

That gets me pissed, but it also gets me thinking how this whole place is messed up past the usual shit in lockup. How I haven't even got a lame-ass public defender to help me out. How nobody even knows where I am.

Maybe it doesn't even matter what Lexi says. Even if she doesn't say shit about me, does that mean they let me go? And if they don't, who's going to care? Who's going to get me out? Eddie? My grandmother? Becca? Who remembers me? Is anybody even thinking about me?

All I left behind at Pelón's place was some clothes and my music. I can already see him swapping my shit for a couple of joints. My backpack is locked up by the cops somewhere. And the pieces I canned, they've probably been tagged over or buffed already. Like it's no work to make me disappear.

"Well, they can't fuckin' erase me," I say out loud.

But I know they can.

I have to laugh to keep from tripping. I toss my cot over and do twenty chin-ups. Bam, bam, bam. I can feel my muscles roaring, getting strong, but it's a strength that doesn't even matter now. I know down to my bones that there's no power on my side. Lexi's got people. Shit, she's got a fancy lawyer in a suit.

Me, all I've got is my own skinny ass and a couple of drawings hid under my blanket.

CHAPTER 37: NOW

It's early morning, before breakfast, when I hear footsteps. I know it's Pakmin's walk. I've been waiting to see him, but at the same time I don't want him to come. After all this time alone in my cell, I don't know if I can take seeing his face like another blank wall in front of me, something all my questions just bounce off of.

I guess I can, though, because when he stands on the other side of my bars, I manage to look him in the eyes.

"Long time, no see," I say.

"There are some things we need to take care of," he says. His face is hard, harder even than I remembered. No feeling in it. Not good. Not good.

The cell opens, and he leads me out toward the conference room. My stomach's doing flips.

"I'm going to be direct, my friend," Pakmin says when we sit down at the table. "You've had more time than we usually allow before calling for a decision, and that's becoming a problem."

"Decision? What kind of decision?"

Pakmin silences me with a hand. "Transfer, release, or otherwise, it makes no difference to us. But if you don't find a way to move on soon, that option will be closed to you."

"You're talking like I wanted to come here, man. Like this is the freakin' Marriott or something. I'm ready to go. Just tell me where to sign."

"It doesn't work like that."

"But you got to admit I been trying hard. I put in my time watching the girl. I read my file real careful." I study his face for clues.

"But that's over now, don't you see?" Pakmin lays his big brown hands flat on the table. His knuckles are hairy, and a too-small wedding ring bites into one of his fat fingers.

"What do you mean? I'm gonna see Lexi again, right? I mean, she's supposed to help me remember, right?" I'm scrambling now, freaked out by the idea of not seeing her anymore, of not knowing what happened. What she's done.

Pakmin shakes his head. "It's over, my friend. Yes, yes, so you helped the girl. But you have to take care of your own situation."

"Helped her? Helped her how? All I know is that her lawyer had her set up to dump lies on me in court. So what happened? What'd she say?" I lean forward and then realize my mistake. Too eager. Too damn eager. Now he's not going to tell me shit.

"Her trial is her trial, don't you see? You've got to help yourself. Your release—you must be the one to make it happen."

"But how?"

"You know what you have to do. Remember." Pakmin locks his eyes on mine.

"I can't, man. I tried, but . . ." I think of the drawings and the dreams. My guts twisted. The thing aching in my chest like a memory that got lost from my brain. I know something, but what? Why can't I remember the right shit?

"I can't do much more for you. You have to try harder, Martín."

"It's Azael."

He ignores me. "Start talking. Let yourself own what you know. Right now." His voice has turned from rough to a kind of low purr, and I can't help nodding.

"I'll try it for you, Pac Man."

He doesn't react to the nickname. He just says, "Do it for yourself, my friend." His voice is hard again; his mouth tight under his mustache, eyes narrowed under his one giant bushy eyebrow. I can see my time running out in his look.

"I was with my homeboys," I say quick, before I can think too hard. "We were cruising, heading toward

Montrose. We were supposed to go scare some punks that was messing with a homie's sister. There was a car . . . we followed it. Then we started fighting in this park, about ten of us and maybe fifteen of them. I was looking out for my—" I stop myself. I was just about to say *brother*, to bring Eddie into this. No way, no way do I want to do that.

"I already know your brother was there. Eddie. Go ahead."

I feel sick. I don't know if it's hearing Eddie's name in Pakmin's mouth or the feeling that Pakmin already knows exactly what I'm thinking. But if he knows what I'm thinking, how come I've got to say anything at all?

"The remembering is for you," Pakmin says, like he's answering my question. "Close your eyes." The purr is back in his voice, and so I do it.

My head starts to clear, and I can see the field almost like I'm there. *Eddie and me are beating down this little show-off from Crazy Crew. I don't have my chain anymore, so I'm scanning the ground for a new weapon. First I see an aluminum bat lying in a patch of brown grass a couple of yards from where Greñas is pounding a guy with a pipe. And then I see something else.*

"Red," I say out loud. "I see red."

My hand closes around the bat. I pull it out of the grass. Then I see it again, something red at the edge of my vision. I turn around, and there's this girl in a red tank top and brown shorts headed toward me.

It's not just any girl. It's Lexi.

She laughs when Cucaracha catches a punch in the jaw from this tall motherfucker, but she just keeps on walking, tits swaying a little under her tank top, mouth twisted. She stops maybe five feet away. "You respect Crazy Crew?" she spits out at me.

"Fuck no! MS-13 controla!" I shout. "Now get out of here, bitch."

She keeps coming, though, and I stick the bat out, push her back with it. "You got no business here. Go play with your fuckin' dolls."

Greñas jerks his chin at me as he charges toward two of their guys. "They brought a bitch? Pinche *posers," he laughs. Then he starts throwing punches.*

"You think this is a game?" I say to her. "We're not fightin' you. Get out of here."

Over her shoulder, I see Cucaracha break away from the guy he's fighting. There's blood streaming from his nose, but he swings a chain, and the tall dude backs off.

Cucaracha points at her and shakes his head. Drops of blood fly in both directions. "A fuckin' ho?"

"You shits don't know who you're messing with," she shouts at him. Then she turns to me and lifts her left fist. She's holding a double-bladed knife by the handle in the middle. Part of me is thinking, that's the knife I drew. Part of me is thinking, only a fool would open both blades. Because like that, even when you're pointing the knife at somebody else, a blade is pointing back at you.

Then she starts swinging it through the air in sideways fig-ure eights. The knife looks meaner in motion, the sun catching on its blades.

Another car pulls up on the Crazy Crew side of the field, and a skinny guy runs toward us, dodging Eddie and weaving between my other homeboys fighting on that side. "You're not supposed to be here, Lex!" the guy shouts. "This ain't your business!"

I open my eyes. I'm shaking all over from the remem-bering. "I never fought a girl. We don't fight girls," I say. "I didn't hurt her, I swear. I didn't hurt her. And the other guy—I didn't—I haven't—I never killed nobody."

Pakmin is shaking his head. "You still don't understand."

The way he looks at me, I think he knows that I'm lying. I killed Pájaro, didn't I? He wouldn't be dead if it wasn't for me. I shake the thought away.

"You're running out of time," Pakmin says. "You've got to keep going. Your eyes, you need to close them."

I do what he says. And as I close my eyes, I feel that I'm also obeying something inside of me. It's like at the same time that Pakmin's across the table from me, he's also in me. He's making me remember from the inside.

She turns, and her hair whips around her face. "I don't need your help, Cartoon!" she screams. "I got this!"

While she's looking away, I give her a little push with the bat. She almost loses her balance, and one of the blades scrapes against her arm. It's a shallow cut, but blood beads up in a line on her tan skin. I think, fuckin' fool ho, one little shove and you cut yourself. I hear Eddie laughing from somewhere.

She stares at me, licks the blood from her arm, then laughs. Her mouth twists around words. "You'll regret that," she hisses. There's a drop of blood at the corner of her mouth.

"Not my fault, puta. You cut your own self," I say, laughing. "That's the problem with toy knives and bitches who don't know how to handle them." Then I turn to meet the fool coming my way. Him and his crew are the reason I'm here, not some girl. He has a chain, but my feet are planted, and the bat swings easy and smooth. I'm ready.

"Get this bitch under control so we can fight like fuckin' hombres," I shout.

He ignores me. "Give me the knife, Lexi, and get the hell out of here!" He grabs her arm, but she pulls away, kicking at him.

I toss the bat on the ground to prove that I'm not fighting till she's gone. "This is a joke," I say. "She's the best you got?"

Then I hear Eddie shouting, and I'm spinning around to see if he needs me. I'm done with these two, anyway, ready to leave them to their puppy-love fight when—

I lurch forward and puke. It's like Pakmin knew this was coming because the trash can is already right there between me and the table. There's no food in my stomach, and the vomit burns the back of my throat. I'm cursing all the times I thought I wanted to get my brain straightened out, to get this DVD to quit freezing and skipping. I don't want this. I don't want to know any more. But I can feel the pain spreading from the center of my chest all the same, a pain that wants to take over. A pain that is its own kind of knowing. I throw my head down toward the trash can and spit up another stream of stinging acid.

When I look up, Pakmin meets my eyes. "It's normal," he says quietly, handing me a paper towel. He gives me a second to mop off my mouth then says, "I can't give you much more time, Martín."

I'm so scared I don't even tell him to call me Azael. I just fall back into the remembering. And the pain.

I'm turning away from them when I see a flash of red. Somehow she's in front of me, and something explodes in my chest. I step back, stumble.

For a second, she just stands there, staring at me. "You fucked up," she says. "You really fucked up." She tosses her hair like we're at the mall, but the knife is still clenched in her fist.

One of the blades is halfway folded in and dripping with blood. I watch the red slide down toward the handle. I think, she cut herself. I think, that's a lot of blood.

Then I touch my chest.

When I pull my hands away, they're covered in blood.

"What?" I start to say. "What?" Then I can't speak. My hands go back up to my chest, trying to fix what's messed up, because parts of me that are supposed to stay inside are up against the world, the air, the park, all this. My blood is escaping, and the world is climbing into me through my chest.

I give up on keeping my insides safe. I hold a hand out, taking a step toward her. I want to ask her something, but I can't. I grab her arm. When she pulls it away, it is streaked with blood.

Then she turns and runs. The red of her shirt pulses. The knife blades flash in the sun as she pumps her arms.

All of a sudden everything is too bright, and I need to close my eyes. When I do, the pain in my chest is the only thing that's real. The pain is a room that I walk into. I stand inside it. I am six years old, waiting at a broken window and calling for Mami, then Eddie, then Mami again.

I open my eyes to the unbearable brightness one last time. I see my hands covered in blood. These are my hands. This is my blood.

I feel myself start to fall.

"No!" I cry out. "It's not true!" I pull up my shirt to show Pakmin my chest. No scar.

"You don't need me to tell you," Pakmin says.

"How'd you get this shit into my head?" I'm trembling. I still feel the ache in the center of my body like when I had my eyes closed. I stare at him, almost begging now. "What is this place? What the hell is this place?"

"You decide, my friend. But you'd better be fast." He stands up, and I know he's done with me.

• • •

Back in the cell, I drop onto my cot. I'm still shaking. I grab the breakfast tray and throw it against the wall. Globs of oatmeal dribble down the concrete. The orange juice carton lands with a thud by the sink. Did they pump last night's applesauce full of some crazy no-taste, fake-memory drug? They could, right? They can do anything.

Or am I still sick, tripping from a fever? Are they trying to poison me?

The questions skitter like cockroaches through my head. They don't stick around long enough for me to make sense of anything. I feel like I might puke again, so I press my forehead against the clammy cinder block wall. Once the feeling passes, I reach down and pull my black book and the papers out from under the mattress. Reading is better than thinking, even if I've read it all before.

Only it turns out that I haven't. Because when I look at the article that used to have shit blacked out, the one from June 12, the words that were missing before jump out at me. I read the first sentence. "Martín 'Azael' Arevalo, 15, was stabbed in a gang fight yesterday in a Montrose-area park."

I stare at the words, but they don't make sense. I think of that explosion of pain in my chest when Pakmin made me close my eyes, but I can't get the words to connect up with what I felt. Stabbed? The word is like one of Regina's stickers after she played with them too much. When I try to press it onto what I remember, the edges of the word just curl up, and it falls off.

I choke back more vomit and keep reading. "Gang violence broke the peace yesterday around 2:00 P.M., leaving fifteen-year-old Arevalo dead on the sidewalk, with a four-inch stab wound in his chest." I want to flush the newspaper clipping right down the toilet, but I stare at the words instead, trying to make sense of them. This is some kind of trick. A game. Because I'm right here. They can put all kinds of shit in print, but that don't make it true. Somehow they made it look like this happened to me so they could put me in here.

Then I unfold Becca's letter. *I can never be yours*, she said. *Never.* I throw the letter down, but it's too late. When I see NEVER there in Becca's girly handwriting, I just know. Even though it doesn't make sense. Even though this is all wrong. I know what I know.

Becca didn't quit on me. I quit on her.

I reach for the newspaper page that was blank before. While I look at it, while it's right there in my hands, real as anything, words start to appear. A picture of me, too, one I took of myself with Pelón's cell phone.

I know exactly what's in front of me. An obit. And it's mine.

```
MARTIN "AZAEL" AREVALO, 15

June 16, 2011

    Arevalo died as he lived: in the streets and
separated from his family.

    The 15-year-old was stabbed to death last
Wednesday, June 11, in a gang fight that broke
out in a Montrose dog park around two o'clock
in the afternoon. Numerous members of both
```

gangs have been questioned. Police have taken a 17-year-old white female into custody.

Arevalo is survived by his brother, Eduardo; sister, Regina; father, Manuel; and other relatives. His mother Rosa died shortly after the birth of his sister Regina, and his father has lived in El Salvador since being deported from the U.S. a year ago.

Arevalo and his brother seem to have slipped through the cracks of Houston's social system. After federal agents arrested their father, CPS failed to bring the boys into state custody. The boys lived on the streets, occasionally staying with relatives, but usually drifting between friends' apartments. They both became involved in Mara Salvatrucha, or MS-13, a Los Angeles-based Salvadoran street gang.

Friends and family remember Arevalo as "sweet." His girlfriend Becca Ramirez said, "He was trying real hard to go straight. He'll never be forgotten."

Arevalo's body was transported to El Salvador for burial because his father is not permitted re-entry into the United States. Services

will be held for Arevalo at noon on Saturday
in the Iglesia de Santa Lucía, Santa Ana, El
Salvador.

I want to cry or scream when I see my name there. I want to, but I can't. Because now that I know, I feel like I've known all along, like Tigs was telling me, like Gabe's crazy blue eyes were telling me, like Pakmin's mustache was telling me, like the wall of the cell was telling me, like Lexi's pen was telling me. It was all there.

I slide down onto the floor of my cell, shaking even harder now. My knee knocks against the concrete. I think I might be crying. I don't want my name spray-painted on the sidewalk. I don't want any "R.I.P. AZZ" messages that will just get canned over.

But I can't do anything about that now, can I? Can you change anything once you're dead? I think of Pakmin telling me, "If you don't find a way to move on . . ." All of a sudden I'm feeling every bad thing I ever did like lead in my shoes.

I've got to do something before it's too late.

I grab the pencil from under my mattress. I clench and unclench my fist around it. What can I do? No way am I going to write some message warning my homeboys about how they can end up, because they already know. I knew, too.

Words are no good for me, anyway. So I pull my black book out and turn to the last page, the one I've been saving, and start drawing. Not thinking, just drawing. Not thinking that probably by now every wall I canned has been buffed out or sprayed over with somebody else's tag. Not thinking that I ain't never going to touch Becca's skin again. Not thinking of Regina and Eddie and Pops burying me in the El Salvador I never got to see. Not thinking about Pájaro or whether he's in a cell like this somewhere. Not thinking about Lexi lying on a court-room stand and turning my name blacker than it was already. Not thinking none of that. Just drawing.

First I draw Lexi. Her face is angry but also afraid. Like she was losing everything at the same time as me, like the knife between us was changing everything for her, too. The sketch is in gray because all I've got is pencil, but in my mind I see color. The red of her shirt and the fleck of blood on her lip, the grass in clumps of scorched brown, the shiny blue of Eddie's football jersey.

Then I draw Lexi's knife, but as my pencil flies over the page, the knife comes out different. The double blades tilt up and spread into wings like some kind of crazy street butterfly. The same thing happens when I try to draw chains and pipes and bricks and knives into the hands of my homeboys in the field. The weapons all turn into butterflies. My boys are surprised, pissed even, but they start to look up into the sky as those butterflies get away from them. Maybe somehow that means they're thinking of me. Not the me that's lying on the sidewalk with Eddie grabbing my shirt, his hands shiny with my blood. Not that split-open body, but the me that's already gone from it. Maybe my boys will think of me as they feel their hands go empty. Maybe they'll give up on the rumble. Or maybe they'll just think, *shit*, and start fighting with their fists.

I'm drawing so fast now that my hand aches. Then the ache starts to melt away into something else, an even bigger pain throbbing from the center of me. It turns out that being dead is a lot like being alive—the harder you think about it the less it makes sense.

So I draw. I draw without worrying about what difference it'll make; I draw because the pencil is in my hand. I draw, and I feel all the Azzs I've been, all my choices nested together inside me like the layers of an onion. My pencil is flying because that's how it is: you choose and you choose and you choose, and that's your life. That's what you are.

Lexi and me, we're not that different. I picture her buying the knife, and I know just how it is. You take that knife like it's nothing. You choose the knife, but you always figure that you've got time left to choose the butterfly later.

The pencil is still in my hand, but I'm not drawing anymore. The scene is just about finished. We're all there—Lexi, me, Eddie, Pelón, all the others. Stupid as shit, but alive and free under these clouds of butterflies.

As I stare at the drawing, time changes from something that moves to something that's pressing in on me hard, holding me still. It's getting harder and harder to move. All I do is blink, but it takes forever for my eyes to open again. The moment stretches on and on. I close my eyes again, and the cell disappears, not just out of sight for a second, but erased by darkness. Darkness and a throbbing silence. No knives, no butterflies.

Somehow I know that this dark stillness could be it for me. It's not so bad, kind of calm and safe. But to break free, to climb out and see what's next, that's something, too. I make one final effort, open my eyes, and sign my name to the last page in my book.

I let go of the pencil, and my eyelids fall shut. The darkness isn't so heavy now. I think I smell cinnamon. Cinnamon, and something sharp and clean. Spray paint? I don't know for sure, but maybe being out of pages doesn't mean I'm done making a mark.

EPILOGUE

SURPRISE COURTROOM CONFESSION IN ALLEN TRIAL

September 27, 2011

Houston, TX – Yesterday's surprise on-the-stand confession from 17-year-old Alexis Allen stunned listeners in the courtroom—including her own attorney.

Allen is on trial for the June 11 murder of Martín "Azael" Arevalo, a 15-year-old member of the gang MS-13. Although Allen admitted to stabbing Arevalo at the time of her arrest, her counsel has maintained that she acted in self-defense.

But when defense attorney Lucas VanVeldt asked her to describe what happened the day of the stabbing, Allen apparently broke from the script. After a lengthy pause, with her eyes shut tightly and her hands clasped as if in prayer, Allen said, "I knew what I was doing when I stabbed Azael. He wasn't trying to hurt me when I did it. He wasn't even holding the bat."

Even as her own lawyer was objecting to her testimony, Allen continued her tearful account. "I wanted to prove to my homeboys that I was strong. It happened so fast. I never thought I could kill someone. My mind was blurry from the bars I took ["bars" is the street name for the sedative drug Xanax], but I know what I did. I went against God and everything that's right, and I killed him. And I am so, so sorry."

When she finished speaking, Allen opened her eyes and looked straight at a woman who was later identified as her grandmother. Allen smiled shakily, then began to sob.

Allen's confession represents a major upset for the defense. Her attorney insisted that Ms. Allen was not well at the time of her testimony. The judge agreed to adjourn court for two days, and Allen is currently undergoing a psychiatric evaluation.

The lead prosecuting attorney, Michelline Camacho, spoke to the press as she exited the courtroom yesterday. "There's no doubt in my mind that jurors will find her guilty," she told reporters. "What we have here is a case of conscience at work, and I'm deeply grateful for the family of the victim that the truth has finally come to light. That the defendant herself told the truth, well, that makes it all the more meaningful." When asked about the possibility of a plea bargain, Ms. Camacho shook her head.

Allen's counsel turned down two no-jail plea bargains prior to going to trial.

Irving Griggs, a law professor at the University of Houston who has been following the case closely, explains that while Allen's confession will likely lead to a guilty verdict, jurors are sure to be affected by her words. "You just don't see that kind of sincerity on the stand, not when speaking the truth means putting your own skin on the line. Nobody in the courtroom breathed while she was talking. It was unbelievable."

Griggs and other legal experts expect a more lenient sentence than Allen would otherwise have received if found guilty of murder. Still, she will likely face a much harsher sentence than if she had accepted the plea bargain offered by the prosecution earlier this month.

Unless the defense elects to call additional witnesses, the case will likely go to jury when the court reconvenes on Friday.

AUTHOR'S NOTE

The Knife and the Butterfly is a work of fiction. The inspiration for the novel, however, came from an actual event. On June 6, 2006, Ashley Benton stabbed Gabriel Granillo with a double-bladed knife during a gang fight in a Houston park.

In a statement to the police the following day, Benton asserted, "When he started to run away, that's when I caught him." She also laughed repeatedly and described eating at a Mexican restaurant after the stabbing.

But when Benton was tried for murder in 2007, her lawyers argued that she struck Granillo in self-defense. That trial ended with a hung jury, and Benton later accepted a plea bargain. In exchange for pleading guilty to aggravated assault with a deadly weapon, she received five years of probation. After two years, a judge suspended the remaining probation, and Benton was free to go on with her life.

Of course, by now you know that *The Knife and the Butterfly* is not a story of courtroom drama; the trials that interest me most take place in the human heart.

As I wrote *The Knife and the Butterfly*, Azael and Lexi quickly took on a life quite independent of the "real" Granillo and Benton I read about in the papers. I had to grow into the writer who could tell Azael and Lexi's story, a story that is much darker—and more hopeful—than I ever imagined starting out. I have done my best to portray faithfully the complex loyalties, relationships, and insecurities of teens on society's fringe.

I learned a great deal about MS-13, which has been described by some as the world's most dangerous gang, but I focused on the particulars of MS-13's activity in Houston. I also researched street writers (graffiti artists) to understand what making a mark on the city's face might mean to a teen like Azael. Finally, I explored the particularities of the Salvadoran immigrant community in Houston. Spanish speakers will notice the occasional use of "vos" by Azael's older relatives, which is characteristic of Salvadoran Spanish, while Azael's and his peers' speech reflects the influence of other dialects.

Above all, I wanted to show Azael and Lexi's world as much more than just a patchwork of crime and violence. In addition to the very real threat of their circumstances and the danger of poor choices, I hope to have captured these two teens' vulnerability and their potential for re-demption. For teens like Lexi and Azael, the knife is often easier to find than the butterfly, but that doesn't mean the butterfly isn't there.

ACKNOWLEDGMENTS

Much gratitude to the following professional rock stars: my agent, Steven Chudney; my editor, Andrew Karre; and Lindsay Matvick, Elizabeth Dingmann, and all the others at Lerner who work behind the scenes to make great books happen. I'm also grateful to Blythe Woolston for blazing trails and sharing her wisdom.

A special thank you to the turn-around scholars of my freshman English summer school class at Davis High in Houston. I started finding Azael's voice while we were writing together back in 2007, and you told me that you wanted to hear more of it. I'm glad you put me on the right track.

To my writing group, thanks for reading the manuscript (twice). To Alisa, thank you for the friendship that makes writing seem possible all over again every time we talk.

To my families from Kilgore, El Paso, Houston, Denver, and beyond, thank you for believing in my writing. Special thanks to my parents, who can find redemption anywhere and who support me in everything, and to my brother, Justin, who never, never leaves me in the lurch.

And most of all, thank you to my boys for all the days and nights you shared me with my writing. Arnulfo, thank you for reading and for listening. I still can't believe my luck. Liam, thank you for your jokes, your laughter, and your *besos*. You two are the best part of my every day.

ABOUT THE AUTHOR

Ashley Hope Pérez grew up in Texas and served in the Teach for America Corps in Houston. She has worked as a translator and is completing a PhD in comparative literature. She spends most of her time reading, writing, and teaching college classes on vampire literature and Latin-American women writers. *Kirkus* called her first novel, *What Can't Wait*, "*Un magnífico* debut." Ashley lives in Indiana with her husband, Arnulfo, and their son, Liam Miguel. Visit her online at www.ashleyperez.com.